"I'm not going anywhere." For the first time in the past couple of hours, emotion played on her face as she lifted her chin with stubborn defiance.

"That was one of the conditions of me bringing you back here," Troy replied.

"I'm changing the condition."

Troy swallowed a sigh of impatience. He'd hoped she'd be reasonable, but apparently that wasn't going to be the case. "I promised your father that I'd keep you safe," he said.

"I am safe. I'm in my own home." She stood abruptly. "You don't have to worry about me. It was nice seeing you again, Troy, but your services as a bodyguard are no longer required."

CARLA CASSIDY

HEIRESS RECON

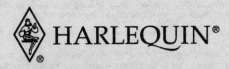

TORONTO • NEW YORK • LONDON
AMSTERDAM • PARIS • SYDNEY • HAMBURG
STOCKHOLM • ATHENS • TOKYO • MILAN • MADRID
PRAGUE • WARSAW • BUDAPEST • AUCKLAND

Recycling programs
for this product may
not exist in your area.

ISBN-13: 978-0-373-69407-5

HEIRESS RECON

Copyright © 2009 by Carla Bracale

www.eHarlequin.com

Printed in U.S.A.

ABOUT THE AUTHOR

Carla Cassidy is an award-winning author who has written more than fifty books for Harlequin and Silhouette Books. In 1995, she won Best Silhouette Romance from *Romantic Times BOOKreviews* for *Anything for Danny*. In 1998, she also won a Career Achievement Award for Best Innovative Series.

Carla believes the only thing better than curling up with a good book to read is sitting down at the computer with a good story to write. She's looking forward to writing many more books and bringing hours of pleasure to readers.

Books by Carla Cassidy

*Cheyenne Nights
†The Recovery Men

CAST OF CHARACTERS

Brianna Waverly—A beautiful heiress who has become a target.

Troy Sinclair—It was supposed to be an easy job for this reluctant bodyguard, but it doesn't take him long to realize he might be in over his head.

Brandon Waverly—Have his ruthless business practices put his daughter at risk?

James Stafford—How far will the angry activist go to stop Brandon Waverly?

Kent Goodwell—Brianna's high school sweetheart. Had his young love for her transformed into something obsessive and disturbing?

Heather Waverly—Brianna's stepmother. Did she harbor a secret resentment toward her beautiful stepdaughter?

Sandy Cartwright—One of Brianna's employees at Pampered Pets, the animal shelter Brianna owns.

Mike Kidwell—The manager of Pampered Pets. What secrets did the quiet man possess?

Prologue

The music in the club pulsed inside Brianna Waverly as she made her way toward the bar. Following close at her heels was her bodyguard, Curt McCain. The man was as big as a house, making her feel even more diminutive than her five-foot height.

As she threaded her way through the throng of people her name was called from here and there. "Bree! Over here!"

She turned to see one of Hollywood's up-and-coming actresses waving wildly at her. She grinned and waved back but continued her trek forward.

Curt hated the nights she decided to go clubbing, complaining that it was difficult to discern between normal Hollywood types and freaks. But the people she met in the clubs were the same she'd talk to later about making a donation to her animal shelter in Kansas City. Networking was nothing if not a fine art, and Bree had made something of a living at it.

The bartender grinned at her as she reached him. "The usual?" he asked.

She nodded. The usual was a club soda with a twist of lime. While most of the others around her got drunk and stupid, Bree stayed clearheaded and smart.

Curt stood several feet away from her, the glare on his bulldog face enough to keep any sane person away. She'd told him a million times that he took the job too seriously. Mostly she needed him to navigate her through a crowd of eager paparazzi bent on getting a photo of heiress and party girl Bree Waverly.

With drink in hand, Bree turned and surveyed the scene. Everyone who was anyone eventually wound up at Oscar's at the end of a long night of partying. The club was the newest, hottest scene in Hollywood.

Lights flashed and swirled on the dance floor, splashing the gyrating bodies with vivid color. She took a sip of her drink and tried to find the joy, the heart-pounding excitement that used to possess her whenever she entered one of these places. But the joy wasn't there. Lately, nothing in Hollywood made her happy.

She'd just as soon be back in her villa, wearing her nightgown and working on the last of the details for the upcoming adoption day at the Kansas City shelter.

A scream from behind pulled Brianna from her thoughts. Before she could turn around to see the cause, Curt yelled her name and threw himself at her. She crashed backward and down, vaguely aware of people screaming. As her head connected with the floor, she saw the spinning lights of the dance floor inside her brain—then nothing.

Chapter One

"I want you to repossess my daughter."

Troy Sinclair stared at the man who had uttered the words, wondering if Brandon Waverly had lost his mind. "Excuse me?"

Brandon leaned back in the overstuffed chair at the huge mahogany desk. Behind him the wall was decorated with framed photos of him with the mayor of Kansas City and other dignitaries, not only locally but also nationally known.

Brandon Waverly was a wealthy, successful real estate developer and builder in the Kansas City area and a close friend of Troy's father, but at the moment none of that mattered to Troy as he wondered just when Brandon had gone crazy.

"Sir, Recovery Inc. isn't into repossessing people," Troy began, then paused as Brandon waved a hand to stop him from whatever he had been about to say.

"I know your company gets back boats and planes and whatever else people decide not to pay for, but I also know there are times when you aren't exactly orthodox in your business practices and you go above and beyond for a worthy cause. My daughter is a worthy cause."

Brandon leaned forward, his blue eyes filled with a torment Troy couldn't begin to understand. "Perhaps I used the wrong word. What I want you to do is take my daughter someplace safe for a couple of days."

"And why would I want to do that, sir?" There was no question that Troy was intrigued even though he didn't want to be. Troy had only met Brianna Waverly once, when he'd been fifteen years old and she'd been ten.

He remembered little about her other than she'd been a pretty little girl with big blue eyes and pale blond hair, but now everyone "knew" of Bree Waverly, Hollywood party girl and a favorite target of the paparazzi.

Troy had no desire to have anything to do with Brianna Waverly, no matter what the circumstances. Still, he would give Brandon the respect of letting the man finish what he had to say.

"As you might know, I'm in the middle of a huge project," Brandon explained. "I'm developing a new mini-mall on some property north of town. Unfortunately not everyone has been happy to see it going in. We've just started construction, and we've already had some vandalism and threats from people who don't want to see retail stores in the middle of farmland.

"There's a meeting planned for Wednesday night, a meeting at which I hope we're going to mend some fences. I'm offering some concessions to the residents that I hope will move things forward, but in the meantime it all has suddenly gotten particularly ugly."

He opened the top drawer of his desk and pulled out a manila envelope. "I received this at my home this morning." His thick fingers shoved the envelope toward Troy. "Go on, open it."

Reluctantly Troy unfastened the flap and pulled out the contents. There were a total of five photos cut from a popular tabloid. Each depicted the lovely Brianna Waverly doing what wealthy heiresses do best—going into a popular club, getting out of a limo, sipping a cocktail and sticking out her tongue at a photographer.

The only thing remarkable about the photos was the stunning beauty of the woman and the bright red, angry X slashed through each one. There was no doubt that the pictures were intended as some sort of threat.

The photo captions were as provocative as the woman. MIDWEST HEIRESS DRINKS UNTIL DAWN. BEAUTIFUL BREE AND HER BODYGUARD. WAVERLY HEIRESS WALKS THE WILD SIDE.

Troy felt a sinking sensation in the pit of his stomach. "Isn't your daughter in California? That's a long way from your problems here."

Brandon pulled yet another tabloid from his top

drawer. Troy stared at the headline. BEAUTIFUL BREE ATTACKED, BODYGUARD STABBED.

"This happened two nights ago at a club called Oscar's. Curt, Brianna's bodyguard, was stabbed but the intended victim was Brianna. He's still in the hospital and doing just fine. Meanwhile Brianna is arriving here in town this afternoon for a two-week visit," Brandon replied with a frown. "I'm afraid somebody went after her to get to me, and I'm worried about her being here unprotected. Please, Troy. I'm begging you as a friend of your father's, as one ex-Navy brother to another."

Troy sighed. He didn't want to do this, but he knew he was going to, because Brandon was an old family friend and because he'd served his country with distinction years ago as a Navy seaman. As an ex-Navy SEAL, Troy couldn't turn his back on the man.

"How exactly is this going to work?" he finally asked, ignoring the gut instinct that told him he was about to make a huge mistake.

THE MEETING LASTED for another hour, then Troy left the downtown Waverly offices and headed to the north side of town where his company, Recovery Inc., was located.

The early September air still held the heat of summer, but he scarcely noticed the temperature as his head whirled with everything Brandon had asked of him. Brandon Waverly hadn't lost his mind, but obviously Troy had when he'd agreed to be a part of the madness.

The Recovery Inc. office was housed in a strip mall, flanked by a pizza place on one side and a beauty shop on the other.

Boredom, he thought as he drove. That's part of what had driven him to agree. Business had been slow the last month after some bad publicity had been generated from a mess his partner, Micah Stone, had gotten into. The mess had been cleaned up, and Micah had found the love of his life, but the residual effect had been that things had been far too quiet the last couple of weeks.

He thought of the photos he'd just seen of Brianna Waverly. There was no question that she was beautiful, but she reminded him of somebody from his past and those memories were ones he rarely visited because they hurt too much.

If he was lucky, one of his partners would talk him into calling Brandon and telling him he'd changed his mind. He parked in front of the business, a surge of pride swelling in his chest as he saw the discreet sign that read Recovery Inc.

Three years ago when he and two of his Navy SEAL buddies had opened the business, they'd never dreamed of how successful they'd become. For Troy the success was particularly welcome because he'd done it on his own, without his family money.

As he entered the office he found Micah and Lucas

in their usual places—Lucas sprawled on the tasteful sofa, and Micah reared back in the chair at his desk.

"I see you're both hard at work," he said dryly.

Lucas sat up and stretched with arms overhead, the motion tugging his T-shirt up to expose his flat, tanned abdomen. "I might look like I'm half-asleep, but actually my mind is whirling to solve all the world's problems."

Micah snorted. "Yeah, and occasionally for the last hour or so, I've actually heard the snoring sounds his mind makes when it works."

Troy grinned and walked across the room to his desk. "I just left Brandon Waverly's office, and he has a job for me," he said.

"I hope it's something exciting," Lucas replied.

"It's a one-man job. He wants me to take his daughter, Brianna, and put her someplace safe for a couple of days."

Micah frowned. "Brianna Waverly. Isn't that Bree Waverly?"

Troy nodded and Lucas released a low whistle. "That is one hot woman."

"Yeah, if shallow and plastic is your type," Troy replied. He told them everything that Brandon had said and about the clippings the man had received earlier that morning.

"How does he know it isn't some garden-variety California freak who sent the clippings and tried to get to her in the club?" Micah asked. "Any creep might have developed some kind of fixation on Bree Waverly. It happens all the time in Hollyweird."

"Brandon seems fairly certain that the threats are directed at him because of the shopping mall project he's involved with at the moment." Troy leaned back in his chair, wishing one of them would tell him the whole idea was stupid. "But he thinks they'll try to hurt his daughter to get at him."

"There's always the safe house," Micah suggested. "You could take her there." The safe house was a farmhouse north of the city proper that the company owned to be used for just these kinds of jobs.

"Or if you want to get her out of town, I've got that little fishing cabin south of here. It would be a perfect place to stash her for a few days," Lucas said. "I haven't been there this year so the windows are boarded up and it's probably dusty as hell. You know it's close quarters, and it's sure nothing fancy."

That was an understatement. In truth the cabin was downright rustic. A woman like Bree Waverly, who was accustomed to the finest things and the world revolving around her axis, would probably take one look around and break out in hives.

Troy wasn't sure why that particular thought gave him a bit of pleasure.

Lucas shrugged. "Compared to some of the jobs we've had, this sounds easy enough. All he's asking of you is that you be a glorified babysitter for a couple of days."

Lucas was right. It sounded easy enough. So why were all of Troy's instincts screaming at him to run as far away as fast as possible from this particular job?

BRIANNA WAVERLY was happy to be home. Even though she'd lived in Hollywood for the past six years, Kansas City, Missouri, was the place she thought of as home, and after the events of the last couple of days, she was even happier to be here.

There were times when it was hard for her to believe that the daughter of a Kansas City developer had become a "name" in Hollywood. All it had taken was her showing up at some of the hot spots and catching the eyes of several paparazzi. Suddenly her pictures had been in the tabloids and the girl from Kansas City was a star.

She stood in front of the full-length mirror in her childhood bedroom to check her appearance one last time before going downstairs for dinner.

She would have preferred a quiet evening spent with just her father and her stepmother, Heather. But the minute Brianna had walked through the front door, Heather had informed her that Brianna's father had invited a business associate to join them for dinner.

Tucking a strand of her long, straight blond hair behind her ear, she turned away from the mirror. She'd been hoping to have a little time alone with her dad this evening to tell him of the life-altering decision she'd made, but as she looked at the clock on the nightstand she realized she'd probably have to wait until the next day for the heart-to-heart chat.

She smoothed a hand down the front of the designer dress she'd bought the day before and thrown into her suitcase at the last minute. The little black number was sinfully short and fit her slender curves as if it had been designed specifically for her. The label would impress Heather, and Brianna's father would predictably ask what animal had eaten the lower half of her skirt.

Knowing that it was getting close to mealtime, she left her bedroom and went downstairs to search for Heather. She found the attractive redhead seated in the formal living room sipping a glass of wine.

"There you are," she said as Brianna entered the room. "Your father is upstairs changing for dinner, and I'm expecting Troy to show up any moment. Nice dress."

"Thanks. Troy?" Brianna walked over to the bar and poured herself a glass of the wine that Heather had opened.

"Troy Sinclair, Grace and Lyle's son," Heather replied.

Brianna sank down on the love seat opposite Heather. "Troy Sinclair. I haven't seen him since I was a kid." She hadn't seen him in years, but she remembered him. At ten years old she'd had a huge crush on the boy with the blond hair and the gunmetal-gray eyes. "He's working for Dad now?"

Heather shrugged her bone-thin shoulders. "I guess so. You know I don't pay any attention to your father's wheeling and dealing. Now, tell me all about what's going on in your life."

Her mother had died when Brianna was ten, and her father had married Heather eight years ago. Brianna had just turned twenty-one; Heather had been thirty.

It had been Heather who had encouraged Brianna to head to California and enjoy her youth, beauty and financial freedom while she could. Heather loved the gossip magazines, and in a bid to please the woman who was now her father's wife, a young and naive Brianna had left Kansas City with the goal of becoming one of the women her stepmother seemed to admire.

It had only been in the last couple of years that Brianna had recognized that her stepmother might have had an ulterior motive for urging Brianna out of the nest and halfway across the country. With Brianna gone, Heather could have her husband's attention all to herself.

The two had only been talking a few minutes when Brandon swept into the room. "There she is!" He held out his arms to Brianna, who instantly jumped up to greet him.

Hugging her father had always been as comforting as hugging her favorite teddy bear, and this time was no different. He wrapped her up and gave her a smacking kiss on the forehead, then released her.

"Did the seamstress forget to add the skirt to that blouse?" he asked gruffly.

She smiled and touched his cheek with her fingers. "I've missed you, Dad."

"I've missed you, too. Are you doing all right?" His sharp blue eyes gazed at her intently. "Curt doing okay?"

She nodded. "I spoke to him right before I got on the plane. They're going to release him in the next day or two." She fought a shiver as she thought of the attack in the club.

Brandon frowned and said, "I can't believe they didn't catch the person responsible."

"It all happened so fast. When I spoke to the police yesterday they said they couldn't get a credible witness statement. According to the people they interviewed in the club, the man who attacked me was a tall blonde, a short bald man and a burly dark-haired man."

"She's safe and she's here now," Heather said. "Let's just put that unpleasantness behind us." Before she could say anything else the doorbell rang.

"Ah, good. That will be Troy," Brandon said. As he left to greet the houseguest, Brianna sat up straighter in her chair. It would be interesting to see what kind of man the boy had grown into.

Hot. That was the first word that popped into her head as Troy Sinclair entered the room at her father's side. His buzz-cut blond hair emphasized lean, elegant features. His broad shoulders, slim hips and long legs were a perfect display form for the dark-blue suit he wore.

Living in Hollywood, Brianna was accustomed to seeing handsome men, but Troy Sinclair radiated an energy that warmed her and sent butterflies dancing in the pit of her stomach. Her reaction to him shocked her. It had been a very long time since any man had made her particularly pleased to be a female.

"Troy, it's nice to see you again," she said. The warmth that had momentarily swept through her vanished as she met his gaze. His eyes were as cold as a gray winter sky.

His head bobbed in a curt nod and he smiled, but there wasn't any warmth behind it. "Nice to see you, too," he said, then turned away from her as Brandon offered him a before-dinner drink. Okay, so the man was hot to look at and apparently very reserved. She sat back down on the love seat.

"We need to make a toast," Brandon said and took Brianna's glass from her. "I'll fill this up for you. Troy, have a seat there next to my little girl."

He smelled wonderful, Brianna thought as Troy sat close enough to her that she could feel the heat radiating from his body. A combination of clean male and a spicy cologne. "I understand you're working for my father. What exactly is it that you do?" she asked.

"I'm an independent contractor," he replied.

"Troy is helping me with a little issue that has come up with the mall development," Brandon explained as he handed Brianna her glass. "And now a toast," he exclaimed as he lifted his own goblet. "To Brianna's visit home and the hope that she knows just how much her old man loves her."

Brianna's heart swelled as she smiled at her father, then took a sip of the drink he'd prepared. Robert, the cook, appeared in the doorway. "Dinner is served," he announced.

Within minutes they were all seated in the dining room. The conversation was light and pleasant, but Brianna felt a simmering tension in the air.

She found herself studying Troy, who sat across the table. He was definitely eye candy and unfailingly polite, but she sensed a faint disapproval wafting from him each time he glanced her way.

"Brianna, honey, we need to have a serious talk," Brandon said as they finished up the meal.

Brianna shot a quick glance at Troy, then looked back at her father. "Okay," she said slowly. "A serious talk about what?"

"Troy isn't just our dinner guest this evening. He's here to do a very important job for me," Brandon said. "I've hired him to take you someplace safe for a couple of days."

"I am someplace safe. I'm home," she exclaimed, wondering what in the heck was going on. "Dad, if this is about what happened at the club the other night—"

"It is, and it's not," Brandon interrupted her. "You know I'm starting work to build on the property next to Precious Pets—" she nodded and he continued "—and a lot of the neighbors aren't happy about it. There have been some threats, and I'm worried for your safety."

"And you think the attack the other night in the club might be about this?" It was difficult to believe that somebody who opposed a business deal in Kansas City would fly all the way to California to hurt her. But, it was equally difficult for her to believe that somebody had hated her enough to try to stab her.

"I think it's possible," Brandon replied. "I find it terribly coincidental that I get threats and suddenly somebody tries to stab you." He leaned forward in his chair. "Just do me a favor. Go with Troy for a couple of days, give me some peace of mind."

"A couple of days?"

Brandon nodded and said, "I hope the heat will die down after a meeting on Wednesday night. Four days, Brianna, that's all I'm asking of you."

With the memory of Curt's stabbing so fresh in her mind and with her father's worry shining from his eyes, there was no way she could protest. She'd do anything in her power for her dad, and four days underground couldn't be that bad. "Okay, I'll go with him."

Once again she gazed at Troy, who had remained silent during this discussion. "Can you at least tell me where we're going?" she asked.

"Don't worry, I'll see that you're taken care of," he replied and smiled. And this time there was just a hint of unexpected amusement in his gray eyes.

Chapter Two

They were in his car by seven-thirty that night and headed for the fishing cabin three hours away. Troy was tense, the muscles in his stomach bunched uncomfortably.

Brianna had looked pretty in her tabloid photos, but in person she was a knockout. Her eyes were bluer, her hair blonder and her features more delicate than any mere photograph could capture.

She was slighter than he'd thought, not tall but very slender. The sexy cocktail dress she wore should be considered a lethal weapon, he thought as he turned onto the highway that would take them south.

"Are we going to the Ozarks?" she asked with a touch of eagerness. "Maybe the Four Seasons? I love that place."

Of course she would love the luxury resort with all its amenities. "No, we're not going that far. We're headed to a place owned by a friend of mine." She smelled delicious and he fought the impulse to roll down his window in an effort to banish the appealing scent.

"I was afraid I was going to have to fight my way through a bunch of paparazzi to get to your dad's front door this evening," he said. "Kansas City must be pretty boring for somebody as accustomed to the limelight as you." He heard the slight mocking tone in his own voice and knew it was an effort to distance himself from her.

"Oh, I'm sure I'll manage to dredge up some dreadful publicity while I'm here," she said with cheerful airiness.

"You won't be dredging up any publicity for at least the next four days," he replied.

"I have to be back in town by Saturday," she said.

"Hot date?"

She crossed her legs. "Something like that," she replied vaguely.

God, she had great legs, and he hated the fact that he'd noticed. He didn't want to be attracted to her, didn't want to find anything appealing about her in any way.

He knew her type. Spoiled and selfish, accustomed to people eager to please her, she was like dozens of other women Troy had known in his life, women he'd chosen to avoid as an adult.

Again he was struck by the scent of her perfume and he wished they were traveling in the airiness of a limo instead of the tight confines of his sports car.

She hid a yawn with the back of her hand.

"The Hollywood fast lane must be catching up to you," Troy said, then felt the weight of her stare.

"You know, that's the second or third thing you've said to me with a bit of a nasty undertone to your voice. I'm just trying to figure out if you work at being a jerk or it just comes naturally?"

By calling him out she surprised him. He shrugged. "It's not anything I consciously work on," he replied.

"That answers my question." She flipped the air conditioner vent to blow more directly toward her face. "So tell me, is this something you do all the time? Play bodyguard?"

"No. I own a company, Recovery Inc. My two partners and I are in the repossession business." He didn't bother to tell her that they were high-stakes players who dealt only in high-stake issues.

"So, you repossessed me."

"Temporarily," he agreed.

"If you don't normally do this kind of work, then why did you agree to do it for my father?"

"Because he's a friend of my parents and because he used to be a Navy man." Troy checked his rearview mirror. At this time of night there were few cars on the road, but he wanted to make sure they hadn't been followed from the Waverly estate by the over-eager press or somebody with more nefarious ideas.

"And you were a Navy man?" she asked.

"Navy SEAL."

"Ah, that explains it."

He glanced at her, her features visible in the light from the dash. "Explains what?"

She flashed him a cheeky grin. "Your buff body."

Troy couldn't remember the last time he'd blushed, but her words filled his cheeks with unexpected heat. He had a feeling that these three hours in the car with her were going to feel like ten, and he didn't even want to think about the next four days.

"Is there a Mrs. Repo Man sitting at home waiting for you?" she asked.

"No," he replied, although he knew the kind of woman he eventually wanted in his life. She would be beautiful, but shy. She'd know the value of a dollar, but would have a giving soul. She'd be an ordinary woman, but extraordinary to him. It was an ideal that he had yet to find, but she was out there somewhere.

Thankfully, Brianna fell silent and stared out the passenger window. Unfortunately, she was only silent for a few minutes. "Do you believe my father's theory that the person who tried to stab me is somehow connected to his business deal in Kansas City?"

"Who knows," he replied. "I suppose anything is possible. Of course, it might have nothing to do with your father and instead might be a by-product of your lifestyle. Women like you sometimes get the attention of creeps."

Once again he felt the weight of her glare. "Women

like me?" She repeated the words in a slow and measured tone. "You don't know me."

"I know everything I need to know about you," he replied.

A woman like Bree Waverly had been the cause of him joining the Navy when he was twenty-three years old. He had expected to marry her, but when a false rumor began swirling that his family had lost their fortune in a stock deal, she'd broken off the engagement. So instead of walking down the aisle, he'd walked into the nearest Navy recruitment office in an effort to forget Holly, the beautiful blonde who had broken his heart.

"Really? And what do you think you know about me?" Brianna asked.

Troy sighed. He wished he'd kept his mouth shut, but that had never been one of his strong suits. He was a straight shooter who rarely hesitated to speak his mind. "I know that you're probably spoiled and love attention. I know that everything in your life has come easily to you. You probably drink too much and take drugs and don't realize you're a train wreck about to happen."

She surprised him with a laugh. "Amazing," she exclaimed.

"What?"

"It's amazing that my father decided to have me repossessed by a judgmental, self-righteous jerk." She laughed again. "This is going to be interesting, repo man. It's definitely going to be interesting to see if we can spend four days together without one of us killing the other."

With this pronouncement she lowered the back of her seat, turned her head to the side and closed her eyes.

SHE MUST HAVE fallen asleep because when Brianna opened her eyes again, the car had come to a stop. She put her seat up and looked around, but the night's darkness prevented her from seeing exactly where they were. The headlights of the car were pointed toward a heavily wooded area but no other structure was visible.

"We're here," Troy said. "Why don't you sit tight and I'll go turn on some outside lights?" He opened the car door and got out.

She nodded as the last sleepiness fell away. She wasn't sure what she'd been expecting when he'd told her they were going to a friend's place, but this definitely wasn't it.

As lights suddenly appeared, she stared with dismay at the little cabin tucked into the woods. Okay, maybe he was right. Maybe she was just a little bit spoiled because she found the idea of spending four days in this boarded-up, dilapidated place appalling.

Troy returned to the car and motioned her out as he opened the trunk. "Is there running water?" she asked, unable to keep her repugnance from her voice.

"Sure," he replied cheerfully. "Although the water pressure leaves something to be desired." He pulled her suitcase from the trunk and placed his smaller black duffle beside it. "I unlocked the front door." He picked up his duffle and headed toward the porch, a jaunty energy in his step. He paused at the doorway and turned back to her. "Are you coming?"

She looked from him to the heavy suitcase she'd brought. "I'm coming," she muttered and grabbed the suitcase handle.

He was enjoying himself, she thought as she dragged the case across the ground toward the porch. He'd judged and condemned her as a carefree, spoiled party girl who lived a life of luxury, and he liked the idea of bringing her to this place where she'd have to carry her own suitcase through the front door.

Buck up, she told herself. If this put her father's mind at ease, then she could deal with anything for four days, even this crappy cabin and Troy Sinclair.

She huffed with the effort to pull the suitcase up the porch and inside the front door. He could have at least helped her through the door, she thought irritably.

The cabin wasn't quite as bad on the inside as she'd expected. She entered a room that served as both kitchen and living room. The furniture was mismatched, as if it had been collected at a thrift store, and the kitchen appliances looked older than her. There were two other doors, one she presumed led to the bedroom and the other to the bathroom.

She dragged her suitcase toward the door she guessed was the bedroom. "I'm going to bed. I'll see you in the morning," she said. "Oh, and by the way, I like my breakfast around tenish."

It was a great exit line meant to get under his skin. Unfortunately, she had pulled her suitcase into the bathroom. With as much dignity as she could muster, she left the bathroom and yanked the suitcase into the bedroom. She ignored his grin of amusement.

Although she expected sleep to be a long time coming in an unfamiliar bed and with the events of the day to mull over, sleep came as soon as she laid her head on the pillow.

SHE AWAKENED SLOWLY, first recognizing someplace in the back of her sleep-addled mind that the bed beneath her wasn't her own. The second thing that came to her attention was the sound of melodic birdsong.

She cracked open an eyelid and stared at the rough-hewn wooden wall in front of her. There was a window directly ahead, but only slender slivers of sunshine danced around the boards that covered almost all of the glass.

The cabin. That's right. She was in the middle of the woods in a cabin that belonged to Troy Sinclair's friend. She was stuck here for the next four days with a man who apparently believed she was nothing more than what the tabloid headlines claimed her to be.

Slinging her legs over the side of the bed, she

grabbed her robe and pulled it around her. Coffee. She could smell the fragrant scent in the air.

Quickly combing her hair with her fingers, she pronounced herself ready to tackle a big cup of java. She opened the bedroom door and instantly spied Troy sitting with his back to her at a small wooden table. At some point while she'd slept he'd removed the boards on the windows, and morning sunshine poured through the streaked glass.

"Ah, the heiress awakens. Coffee is on the counter. Unfortunately, the maid has the day off so you'll have to help yourself." These last words were said with a touch of mocking sarcasm.

"I suppose I can manage to make myself a cup of coffee, but anything more complicated than that is way beyond my capacity," she replied as she walked across the room to the coffeemaker on the countertop.

She poured herself a cup of the brew, then sat at the table across from Troy. He looked as good this morning in a short-sleeved white shirt and jeans as he had the night before in his expensive suit.

"You brought me here on purpose, didn't you? We could have gone to any resort in the country, hidden away in an expensive hotel, but you chose this place just to be difficult."

For the first time, he smiled and the gesture warmed those gorgeous eyes of his. "I thought roughing it would be good for you, build your character. You know, no masseuse, no maid service, no cook."

She took a sip of the coffee. "Ah, we're back to the same thing. You don't know anything about me, and you certainly don't know anything about my character. I'm beginning to find you a bore, repo man."

"I know everything I need to know about you, Bree." He emphasized the name the press had given her.

She took another sip of coffee and eyed him over the rim of her cup. She found his instantaneous, obvious dislike of who he thought she was to be both intriguing and irritating.

She drained her coffee mug and stood, deciding that a shower and getting dressed for the day might make her feel better prepared to take on the next four days.

"I'm going to shower." She walked halfway across the room, then turned back and smiled at him. "I like my eggs scrambled," she said, then disappeared into the bathroom.

If he expected her to be a spoiled brat, then she could act like one. Minutes later she stood beneath a tepid spray of water, her mind flying over the events of the last couple of days.

She knew why it was so easy to exchange verbal insults with Troy; it kept her mind off the fact that her life had become horribly surreal since Curt had been stabbed. There was no question that the knife had been meant for her, that if Curt hadn't acted quickly and taken the knife himself, she would have been wounded or worse.

She'd spent the night of the attack in the hospital

with Curt, waiting while he had surgery to stitch up arm muscles that had been damaged by the cut.

It had almost been a relief for her father to tell her that she'd been threatened because of a business deal he was working on. Before he'd told her his suspicion, she'd been unable to imagine why anyone would want to harm her.

Hopefully, the meeting her father mentioned he had on Wednesday night would resolve this issue and she could get back to her life, a life that would no longer involve L.A. or the paparazzi.

Her life in California was always meant to be temporary. Her one true love was the Precious Pets Animal Haven she owned in Kansas City. She'd hoped to have a chance to tell her dad that she was moving back and taking over the day-to-day running of the business she loved.

She'd already told Mike Kidwell, her manager at the Haven, that she hoped to be working side by side with him in the next couple of weeks.

She shut off the shower and grabbed one of the thin towels to dry off. Hopefully, she'd be able to tell her dad the good news on Thursday. She knew he'd be thrilled with her decision.

In fact, she'd sold her dad part of the land where Precious Pets was located for his new mall. She hadn't considered that her farmer neighbors would be up in arms over the plan for a retail area.

She dressed in a pair of jeans and a T-shirt that

read BREE across the breasts, then brushed out her wet hair and left the bathroom.

Troy stood at the stove taking up crispy bacon. "If you do breakfast really well, I'll see about letting you make me lunch and dinner, as well," she said as she returned to her seat at the table.

He turned to look at her with narrowed eyes. "Don't push your luck, Bree. I'll do breakfast duty and you can do lunch. We can share dinner."

She watched silently as he cracked eggs into a bowl and then scrambled them with a bit of milk. "The last time I saw you, you weren't such a judgmental jerk. What happened since then to change you?" she asked.

"I didn't change and I'm not particularly judgmental." The toast popped up and he grabbed the pieces to butter. "You and I both come from the same background of privilege. Some of us take our wealth and the opportunities it provides us to build something positive with it. Others lead lives of excess and go nowhere."

"And because you've seen a couple of pictures of me in the tabloids, you think you know all about me?"

He scooped up the eggs, prepared them each a plate, then set hers in front of her and joined her at the table.

"You aren't as smart as you look, repo man." She picked up a piece of the toast and took a bite, chewing thoughtfully as her gaze remained focused on him. "If you think those photographs that capture just a second of my life are the total sum of me, then you have a bigger problem than you realize."

He released a small sigh. "Look, I think we've gotten off on the wrong foot. I don't want to spend the next four days trading insults with you. I suggest a truce." He held out his hand to her.

He had a nice hand, one that looked strong and capable. She grabbed it and was surprised by a rivulet of warmth that traveled up her arm. "Truce," she agreed and quickly pulled her hand away.

For the next few minutes they ate in silence. She gazed out the window where the view was of tranquil isolation. Tall trees were grouped closely together with bushes and tall grass at their bases. In the distance the sun sparkled on a large body of water visible between the trunks of the trees.

Actually, four days here didn't seem like such a horrible idea, but she didn't want him to know that's what she thought.

"So, what are we going to do to pass this time in this place?" she asked. "I don't suppose you do manicures."

"Give me a pair of clippers, and I'll do the best I can," he replied.

She winced at the very idea. "I think the only way we'll get along is if you pretend to be my cabana boy and fix me cocktails and hors d'oeuvres."

He grinned at her and said, "I'll consider it after

you put on an apron and pretend you're my maid."
He eyed her curiously. "You know how to fish?"

"Actually I do. When I was little and it was just
me and my dad, he'd take me to Smithville Lake and
we'd sit on the dam and fish on Sunday afternoons.
But I haven't done it in years."

"It's like riding a bicycle, once you've mastered
it you don't ever forget how."

Once again she glanced out the window. The idea
of sitting on a bank with a line in the water was surprisingly appealing. She hadn't realized how scared
she'd been since the attack in the club until now,
when she felt completely safe and protected by the
man who sat across from her.

"How about you wash the dishes and I'll dry?" she
asked when they finished eating.

He looked at her in surprise. "That will work,"
he replied.

Together they stood and carried their dishes to the
sink. He'd just started running water when a cell
phone rang. He quickly shut off the faucet and pulled
the phone from his shirt pocket.

"Sinclair," he said.

Brianna knew instantly that whoever was on the
other end of the line was delivering bad news. Every
muscle in Troy's body stiffened and she could almost
smell the burn of energy that wafted off him.

"Okay. All right. Just sit tight. I'll be back in
touch." He hung up and stared at Brianna, and some-

thing in his look made her heart begin to beat an unsteady rhythm.

"What? Who was on the phone?"

"That was your stepmother. Your father has been kidnapped."

Chapter Three

"Kidnapped?" Brianna stared at him as if the word was as foreign to her as frying onions in a burger joint. "What are you talking about?"

The easy babysitting job had suddenly become more complicated. Troy fought the impulse to take her in his arms. She looked so fragile standing before him, her big blue eyes widened in horror.

"Heather said she got a phone call from someone who told her your father had been kidnapped." He hesitated a moment, unsure how much to tell her, then opted for the whole truth. "The caller told her that if she goes to the authorities Brandon will be killed."

Her gaze darted around his face, as if seeking a sign that this was all a bad joke. "Was there a ransom demand?" she finally asked.

Troy shook his head. "No. They just told Heather to keep her mouth shut if she wants to keep her husband alive."

"You have to take me back. I need to get home." She

looked around wildly. "I've got to get my things together. I need to be with Heather. We need to find my dad." A trembling overtook her as tears filled her eyes.

Troy stepped toward her and grabbed her shoulders, fearing she was about to spiral out of control. "Calm down," he said. "I'll take you back to Kansas City on one condition."

"What condition?"

He released his hold on her shoulders. "The condition is that until we know exactly what's going on, you stay with me in a safe house my company maintains in the city. It's a farmhouse north of town, not far from where your father is building his mall."

"Fine, whatever," she replied.

"Okay, get your things and let's get out of here."

It took only minutes for the two of them to repack their bags, load them into the trunk of the car and get on the road.

"He thought I was the one in danger," she said, her voice thin and filled with worry. "He protected me but he didn't protect himself. Whatever the ransom, I'll pay it. The kidnapper can have every dime I possess as long as he gives my father back unhurt."

"Let's not get ahead of ourselves. We don't know for sure that it's about a ransom."

She looked at him in surprise. "What else could it be about?"

He tightened his grip on the steering wheel and

tried to ignore the tight nerves knotted in his stomach. The fact that the kidnapper hadn't made a ransom demand worried him a lot, but he didn't want Brianna to see his concern.

"Maybe it's about the meeting your dad was supposed to have on Wednesday night," he finally answered. "Maybe the kidnapper believes if Brandon can't make that meeting, the mall development will suffer."

"Maybe," she replied, but he could tell by the dubious tone of her voice that she didn't completely believe it. "But what would that accomplish? Eventually they'll have to let him go."

"We can't really know what's going on until we have more information," he replied. He glanced at the clock on the dashboard. It was almost noon. They wouldn't be back in Kansas City before three. Maybe by then Brandon would show up, and everyone would realize it had all just been a terrible mistake.

"Can't you drive any faster?" she asked impatiently.

"It will slow us down considerably if I get pulled over for a speeding ticket. Just sit back and try to relax until we get you home." He knew how ridiculous it was to tell her to try to relax, but there was nothing else to do at the moment.

"Maybe I should call Heather," she said and dug into her purse to withdraw a sparkly cell phone.

"That probably isn't a good idea," he replied. "She'll

be keeping the line clear in case a ransom call comes in. She promised to call me if anything else happens."

When she dropped the phone back in her purse and fell silent, Troy was grateful. He needed to think. He needed to figure out how to counsel Heather when they got to her house.

He believed, theoretically, that the proper authorities should be contacted when a crime was committed. But he'd never been faced with an actual situation like this.

What if he insisted that Heather call the cops and Brandon was then murdered? He'd have to live with the guilt for the rest of his life. He glanced at the woman beside him. Despite the fact that he believed she was incredibly spoiled and he didn't agree with the way she lived her life, there was no question that she adored her father. Troy didn't want to be responsible for taking Brandon away from his daughter.

He would feel better if they discovered Heather had received a ransom call when they reached her place. At least they would know that they were dealing with a criminal looking for a cash payday. It was much more problematic if a ransom call didn't come in.

Brianna remained silent for the rest of the ride, and Troy couldn't begin to guess what must be going through her head. What surprised him was that she wasn't having hysterics. She wasn't playing the drama queen.

As they pulled off the highway and into her neighborhood, she sat up straighter, her features taut with strain. "Maybe it's all been a sick joke or some kind of a mistake."

"Maybe," Troy agreed, not having the heart to disagree with her. He knew that if that were the case, Heather would have let them know that Brandon was home safe and sound.

Brianna's childhood home was a huge two-story mansion set on two acres of prime property. As Troy turned into the winding circle drive that led to the front door, the knot in his stomach twisted tighter.

On the outside nothing appeared amiss. No police cars were parked in the driveway, no news crews littered the lawn. Apparently Heather hadn't called anyone for help yet.

Brianna was out of the car before he'd shut off the engine. He quickly parked, jumped out of the car and hurried after her.

"Heather!" she cried as she burst through the front door.

The redhead appeared in the doorway of the living room, her eyes swollen and red-rimmed as she twisted a tissue with her fingers. With a small cry, Brianna ran to her and the two women embraced.

"Thank God you're here," Heather said as she released Brianna. "I don't know what I'm supposed to do. I've been afraid to do anything."

"Have you heard anything else? Have you gotten any more calls? A ransom demand?" Troy asked.

"No. Nothing since the first phone call." She motioned them into the living room.

"Have you contacted anyone else?" he asked once they were all seated.

"Only my sister. She's going to be here in a couple of hours to stay with me." Heather dabbed her eyes with the tissue. "And I called Brandon's office to see if he was there, if maybe this is all just a terrible mistake, but his secretary told me he didn't show up for work this morning."

"How did this happen? Do you know where he was taken?" Brianna's voice trembled slightly, and again Troy had the ridiculous desire to pull her into his arms and assure her that everything was going to be fine.

"Apparently somebody was waiting for him when he stepped out of the house this morning. You know your father, the first thing he does after getting dressed and ready for work is walk out to get the morning paper. That's when it must have happened because his car is still in the garage." A sob escaped Heather and she stared at Troy as if he might somehow have the answers to make this all go away. "What do we do now?"

Brianna looked at him, her big blue eyes holding the same appeal as Heather's.

"I need to make some phone calls," he said as he pulled his cell phone out of his pocket. "I want to call my two partners and let them know what's happening, and then I think we need to call Chief Wendall Kincaid of the police department." He hadn't wanted to involve his partners until he'd checked out the situation with Brandon's wife.

Heather shot up from her chair. "No! You can't do that. They said they'd kill him if we contacted the police."

Brianna's eyes grew bigger as she continued to stare at Troy, and he wondered how on earth he'd gotten himself into a position to make such a weighty decision. "We'll give it a couple of hours," he finally said. "We'll see if the kidnapper calls back with a ransom demand. But call or no call, my personal opinion is that it's best to contact the police."

"He's my husband," Heather exclaimed. "And I don't want to do anything to put his life in jeopardy."

"It's already in jeopardy," Brianna said softly. "So there's nothing we can do right now but wait for the phone to ring."

Troy nodded and stood. "And in the meantime, if you'll excuse me, I'm going to make my phone calls." He walked back to the front door and stepped outside to call both Micah and Lucas to let them know what was going on.

If Heather didn't want him to contact the police, then having his partners here was the next best thing. Micah and Lucas could remain here with Heather while he got Brianna settled in the safe house.

Just because Brandon was missing at the moment didn't mean that Troy meant to shirk his duty. Brandon had wanted his daughter under wraps at least until after the Wednesday night meeting, and that's exactly what Troy intended to do.

He was still standing on the porch when Lucas pulled up in his black pickup truck. He had just reached the front porch when Micah roared into the circular driveway and parked his car behind the truck.

Troy quickly filled the two in on what he knew and that Heather was adamantly against calling the police. "Why don't I knock on some doors and see if anyone noticed any suspicious cars or trucks in the area this morning?" Micah suggested.

Troy nodded. "Sounds like a plan. And Lucas, I'd like you to stay with Heather later while I take Brianna to the safe house. I'm hoping a ransom call happens before the night is over. Then we can decide what the next plan of action should be."

The next couple of hours crawled by. Heather's sister arrived and took the distraught Heather upstairs to her bedroom. Micah made the rounds of the neighbors but nobody had seen anything unusual that morning. They waited for the phone to ring as the tension in the air crackled.

Brianna sat curled up on a love seat, looking lost and alone. Her eyes held the torment of her thoughts, and Troy could easily imagine how horrifying those thoughts might be.

By seven o'clock Troy realized there was no point in all of them sitting around waiting for something that might not happen. "Brianna, I want to get you settled in the safe house for the night. Lucas and Micah will let us know if anything happens here, but it's my gut instinct that nothing is going to happen for the remainder of the night."

For the first time in the past couple of hours, emotion played on her face as she lifted her chin with stubborn defiance. "I'm not going anywhere."

"That was one of the conditions of me bringing you back here," he replied.

"I'm changing the condition."

Troy swallowed a sigh of impatience. He'd hoped she'd be reasonable, but apparently that wasn't going to be the case.

"Brianna, your father wanted you someplace safe for a couple of days," he protested. "He didn't want you here in the house, or he would never have hired me to take you off someplace."

She frowned, her eyes radiating pain. "Well, Dad's not here now. Besides, he was afraid somebody might be after me to get to him. They got him." Her voice rose slightly. "They don't need to get me now."

Troy sighed in frustration. He didn't know that the danger to her was over. He couldn't know for sure that the attack she'd suffered in California had been somebody's attempt to hurt Brandon. "I promised your father that I'd keep you safe," he said.

"I am safe. I'm in my own home." She stood abruptly. "You don't have to worry about me. In fact, I'm going to my room and later I'll just go to bed." She moved across the room with a restless energy that was palpable. "It was nice seeing you again, Troy, but your services as a bodyguard are no longer needed."

With these words she left the room.

BRIANNA OPENED her bedroom door and cocked her head to listen. The muted sound of a television was the only noise. It was after midnight and she assumed one of Troy's partners was watching the tube or sleeping in front of it.

The phone hadn't rung throughout the long hours of the night, but the fear inside her had grown to such proportions she could hardly stand it.

Where was her father? Was he still alive? She didn't know what she'd do if something happened to him. She eased the bedroom door open and took a step into the hallway.

She'd never been the kind of woman to sit passively by and do nothing. Despite the fact that she'd told Troy she intended to go to bed, she had to do something or she'd go mad.

Troy. Even though they'd been at odds for much of their time together, there had been several times during the course of the evening when she'd wanted to launch herself into his strong arms. She'd wanted him to wrap her up in an embrace so tight she could hear his heart beating with hers, smell his cologne that, in the space of such a short time, had become oddly familiar and comforting.

She'd seen his sports car pull away a couple of hours ago. She'd noticed only a pickup was left in the driveway.

Instead of heading toward the grand staircase that led down to the foyer, Brianna went the opposite direction to a back, narrow set of stairs that took her to the kitchen. From there she could leave the house and go to the four-car garage in back. Nobody would know she'd left, and she'd be back before morning.

She held her breath as she walked down the stairs, praying that one didn't creak loud enough to stir anyone's interest. If her father had really been taken because of a business deal, then she needed to learn everything she could about that deal. The place to do that was in her father's downtown office.

Before stepping into the kitchen she paused and listened once again. She sure didn't want to encounter Lucas helping himself to a late-night snack or getting a drink of water. She didn't want to have to explain her actions to anyone. She just wanted to do something, anything that made her feel as if she were helping her dad.

There was no indication that anyone was in the kitchen so she stepped into the darkened room and crept to the back door. Four numbers punched into the security panel unarmed the door, and she stepped outside into the warm September air.

A full moon spilled down luminous light as she ran toward the garage. Inside would be the sport-utility vehicle that she always drove when she was home for a visit.

She pulled a set of keys from her jeans pocket, unlocked the garage door and went inside. She was hoping Lucas wouldn't hear her start her car or pull out. She didn't want to worry anybody; she just wanted to do what she felt she needed to do.

She didn't bother turning on the overhead lights. The illumination filtering in the open garage door was enough for her to see her vehicle. She opened the car door and slid inside, then leaned back against the backrest and sighed wearily.

"Where are we going?"

She squealed at the unexpected but familiar deep voice coming from the backseat. She whirled around to see Troy. "What are you doing back there?"

He leaned forward, bringing with him the scent of his cologne that she found so arresting. "I had a feeling you weren't going to stay put tonight."

"I thought I might go down to the local club and do a little dancing," she said with a touch of sarcasm.

"Great, then you don't mind if I ride along." He got out of the back and switched to the passenger seat.

"I thought I fired you," she complained as she started the engine.

He smiled. "You didn't hire me so you can't fire me."

"Then I feel like you're stalking me." The truth was she was a little bit happy for his company.

"Get used to it. Until your dad returns home and tells me my services are no longer required, you're stuck with me. Now, are you going to tell me where we're really going?"

"To my father's office." She backed out of the garage and pushed the button on a remote to lower the garage door. "If this really is about the business deal he's involved with, then I want to know everything there is to know about that deal."

"Why didn't you just tell me that earlier this evening?" His eyes looked almost feral in the light from the dash.

"Because I didn't think you'd let me go. Because I thought you'd insist I sit still like a good little girl, and I can't sit another minute longer. I need to do something." She didn't want him to give her a hard time about this. She was hanging on by a thread, fighting against the fear for her father that threatened to consume her.

He fastened his seat belt. "Then let's get it done."

She flashed him a grateful smile and took off down the street. "How long have you been sitting in the garage?" she asked curiously.

"Since nightfall."

"Am I that predictable?"

He laughed. It was a low, pleasant rumble that momentarily warmed the chill that had possessed her since learning of her father's kidnapping. "Actually, you're that unpredictable. I just had a feeling that you wouldn't be satisfied sitting around with Heather and her sister all night."

"I prefer action to hand-wringing," she replied. Besides, if she sat and wrung her hands for too long she'd start to cry, and there was nothing Brianna hated more than crying.

At this time of night there were few other cars on the road as they headed to the downtown area. She hoped and prayed that somehow they could find a lead hiding in the paperwork in her dad's office.

Brandon's office was on the fifth floor of a ten-story office building. She rang a buzzer and a gray-haired security guard opened the door, his face wreathed in a warm smile.

"Brianna, I didn't know you were back in town," he said as he allowed them entry and then locked the door behind them.

"Got in a couple of days ago, Charlie," she replied.

"Read about your trouble the other night," Charlie said. "Crazy life you lead, Missy."

"I know, Charlie. I know," she replied. "We're going to be a little while in Dad's office."

"No problem. Just holler when you're ready to leave." He went back to the front desk and sat while she and Troy walked toward a bank of elevators.

"You're obviously a familiar sight around here," Troy observed as they stepped into the elevator.

Her heart squeezed painfully tight. "I grew up spending a lot of time here with Dad, and Charlie has been the night security for as long as I can remember."

The doors whooshed closed and the elevator carried them to the fifth floor, where they stepped out and walked the short distance to Brandon's offices.

She used her key to unlock the door and turned on the overhead lights. Directly ahead of them was the receptionist's desk, and behind that desk was the door leading to Brandon's inner sanctum.

She went to that door and opened it, then flipped on the light, conscious of Troy following right behind her.

For a moment the scent in the room caused a stabbing pain to pierce her heart. It smelled like her dad—a blend of his cologne, the mints he loved to chew and the faint aroma of the cigars he occasionally sneaked.

"Are you okay?" Troy asked softly.

She was vaguely surprised to realize that he was sensitive enough to know that being here might be difficult for her.

Nodding, she moved to the desk. "I'm fine," she said, but she wasn't fine. She was scared, more frightened than she'd ever been in her life. "I just want to find something, anything that will make sense of what's happening." She pulled open the top drawer but before she could look at the contents Troy grabbed her by the arm.

"Wait." He moved her to the side and withdrew a large manila envelope from the drawer.

"What's that?" It was obvious by the way he held it close to his chest that he knew what was inside.

His lips compressed together into a thin line as his gray eyes darkened. "It's pictures of you. Your father showed them to me the other day when I was here."

"Pictures of me? Let me see them."

Reluctantly he pulled the photos out of the envelope and handed them to her. "It's why he hired me to watch over you," he explained.

There was no question that the vision of her pictures crossed out with bright red marker was disturbing. She set them on the top of the desk, her fingers trembling slightly. "And Dad thought this somehow had to do with the mall development?"

Troy nodded. "He thought it was a warning that he should shut down his plans for the mall or somebody might try to hurt you."

Without warning she was filled with an enormous sense of grief coupled with a crushing guilt. She dropped the pictures to the top of the desk as tears half blinded her. Not thinking, functioning only on her need to be held, she walked into Troy's arms.

Chapter Four

The next to last thing Troy expected was for Bree Waverly to fall into his arms. The very last thing he expected was his swift, visceral reaction to her being there. The feel of her slender curves and her sexy scent made it hard for him to think. She fit perfectly against him, her rounded body against the harder, leaner angles of his own.

But the sound of her tears as she burrowed her face in the front of his shirt focused him away from the immediate physical pleasure and back to the problem at hand.

She cried only a few moments, then backed away from him and quickly swiped at her tears. "Sorry, I didn't mean to do that," she said.

She dropped into Brandon's chair, looking utterly miserable, and Troy leaned against the desk next to her. "I just feel so guilty," she said.

Troy frowned. "Guilty? Why?"

Leaning her head back, she released a troubled

sigh and once again her eyes shone overly bright with a mist of tears. "I'm the one who talked Dad into the mall. I even sold him the land where he's building. All I thought about was how great it would be for my business."

"Your business?" He thought her business was to show up at extravagant parties and wild clubs and get her picture in the tabloids.

"Precious Pets Animal Haven. It's on the property next to where the mall was supposed to be built. I thought the mall would bring in people who would see my place and maybe come in and adopt a pet."

An animal haven? He tried to wrap his head around this new information. Bree Waverly owned an animal shelter in Kansas City? A tiny crack appeared in the image he'd had of her.

"Brianna, your father is a savvy businessman. He would have never agreed to buy the land and build the mall if he didn't think it was a sound business venture."

The animal shelter was probably some kind of tax write-off for her. Lots of Hollywood types had special charities they funded but didn't have anything to do with.

She eyed the desk. "We need to go through every drawer, every file and see what we can find that might give us a hint as to who's taken my father."

For the next two hours that's exactly what they did. By the time they'd gotten through everything, they had a small pile of papers that pertained to the mall deal. There were several anonymous notes that threatened boycotts and vague disasters. Although they were written in different handwriting, they were all worded the same, which led Troy to believe they were part of a group effort.

One of the letters was signed by a James Stafford. The name rang a bell in Troy's head but he couldn't place it. Besides, he was tired and he knew Brianna was, too. Her pale complexion coupled with droopy eyelids let him know just how exhausted she was.

"We've done enough for tonight," he said. "We're both exhausted and there's nothing more that we can do here."

She nodded and stood, her shoulders slightly slumped forward as if the weight of her own body was too much to bear.

"Brianna, go with me to the safe house," he said. "I'd feel better if you were there until we know what we're up against. It's what your father wanted. It's why he hired me."

"But what if a call comes in at the house or something else happens?"

"Lucas or Micah will call me if anything happens." He reached out and took her hand in his. "Please, don't fight me anymore on this."

"Okay," she agreed. "I'm too tired to argue with you."

He smiled. "I know when to press my advantage. We'll pick up some of your things at the house tomorrow. I can provide you with a clean T-shirt to sleep in for tonight and a new toothbrush to use in the morning."

It was just after three when Troy pulled up in front of the farmhouse owned by Recovery Inc. "It's nothing special, but it's bigger than the cabin I tried to keep you in before."

She gave him a weary smile. "As long as there's a bed, I'll be fine. I just need a couple hours of sleep and then I want to go back through that paperwork again."

Troy picked up the file folder of papers, and together they headed inside the three-bedroom ranch house.

He showed her to one of the bedrooms and retrieved a clean T-shirt from the master bedroom closet. "Try to get some sleep," he said as he gave her the shirt.

"First thing in the morning, I'd like to go to the job site and look around," she said.

"We'll see what tomorrow brings."

Her eyes darkened and he knew what she was thinking, that she hoped tomorrow didn't bring news that her father had been killed.

Despite his exhaustion, sleep didn't come easily. The events of the day replayed in Troy's mind. What would anyone hope to gain by kidnapping Brandon? That's what didn't make sense to him. Sure, his disappearance might slow down the mall project, but even his death wouldn't necessarily stop it altogether.

He finally fell asleep and awakened with the dawn

light filtering through his window. Despite the early hour he grabbed his cell phone from the nightstand and punched in Lucas's number. His partner answered on the first ring. "Anything to report?"

"Nothing," Lucas replied. "Heather and her sister are still in Heather's room, no suspicious phone calls came in and Brianna went to her room early last night and I haven't seen her since."

"She's with me," Troy said. "We're at the safe house. I want either you or Micah to do me a favor and see what you can dig up on a James Stafford. He wrote a nasty letter to Brandon and his name sounds familiar but I can't place it."

"Done," Lucas replied. "I'll call you back as soon as I have some information. And Troy, I really think we should consider calling Kincaid."

"I know," he agreed, thinking of the chief of police. He'd spent the last minutes before falling asleep recognizing that he should have overridden Heather's hysterics and called the authorities immediately.

Troy ended the call and sat on the edge of the bed for several long minutes, contemplating whether to contact Chief Wendall Kincaid.

He was still considering the issue when Brianna joined him in the kitchen just after eight. "Good morning," she said as she beelined for the coffeemaker.

"How did you sleep?" He tried not to notice the subtle sway of her hips as she moved, the way her breasts pressed against the fabric of her T-shirt.

"Surprisingly well," she admitted. She poured herself a cup of coffee, then slid into the seat next to him at the round oak table.

She looked out the window where the view was of farmland, then looked back at him. "Why does your company need a safe house?" she asked.

"We bought this place when we first started our business. We weren't sure exactly what kind of situations we might find ourselves in and envisioned a time when one of us or our clients might need a place to hole up."

She took a sip of her coffee, eyeing him over the rim of the cup. "You three, you do more than repo cars, don't you?"

"For the most part what we do has nothing to do with the blue-collar guy down the street who is a couple of months behind on his car payment. We go after the bigger fish who have bigger toys, and we have contacts that sometimes give us jobs that have nothing to do with the repo business."

"You mean like covert secret mission kind of things?"

He grinned. "I'd love to tell you about it, but then I'd have to kill you."

She laughed, but the laughter was short-lived. "No word from the house?"

"Nothing, and I think we need to call Chief Kincaid." Fear danced into her eyes at his words and he hurriedly continued. "Brianna, Kincaid won't do anything to put your dad at risk, but he has resources we don't have."

She held his gaze, her expression troubled. "I'm so afraid of doing the wrong thing. Let's go check out the job site, then I'll make a decision about contacting the cops."

They left the house at nine. Troy drove Brianna's sport-utility vehicle as she played navigator from the passenger seat. "Turn left at the next intersection," she said as they reached the north edge of the city.

They traveled on a two-lane highway for some distance before she had him turn off again, this time onto a country road. Troy might have enjoyed the pastoral scenery if he wasn't so acutely aware of Brianna's nearness.

He didn't know how it was possible for him to be so physically attracted to a woman he was so certain he had nothing in common with.

She was nothing like the ideal woman he wanted to marry someday, and yet he found himself wondering what her lips would taste like and whether her skin was as soft and silky as it looked.

Last night, in those brief moments he'd held her in his arms, his imagination had been stirred to wonder about things he definitely shouldn't be wondering.

"Up ahead on the right is Precious Pets," she said, breaking the silence that had lingered between them for the last couple of minutes.

Troy slowed the car to a crawl. He saw the sign

by the road first, a big sign depicting a smiling poodle. PRECIOUS PETS—ADOPT A PET TODAY, it read. The establishment itself, a long, low white building, was set back far from the road. The most prominent features on the property were the dozens of large fenced dog runs.

"My mother died when I was three and left me a large inheritance that I received when I turned twenty-one. The first thing I did was buy this land, forty acres. I knew I wanted to build an animal shelter. That's my hot date for Saturday," she said. "Once a year we have a huge open house and adoption day. We've been publicizing the event for the last couple of months."

"Why an animal shelter?" he asked. "I'd figure if you were going to invest in something it would be a designer shoe factory or the hottest purse maker."

"Ah, there you go again, making silly assumptions about my life," she replied. "I've always been an animal lover, and my biggest goal in life has been to rescue those in need and find them good homes."

"That's admirable," he said grudgingly. It would be so much easier to deal with her if she remained in the box he'd tried to put her in, the box of selfish conceit and superficiality.

"Dad's job site is just up ahead," she said as Troy once again stepped on the gas. They hadn't gone far when they reached the site. A trailer sat on the lot along with a couple of bulldozers and other heavy equipment.

Troy parked the car and the two got out. Despite

the fact that it was well before noon, the September sun was warm and the scent of rich dark earth filled the air. A rabbit, startled by their approach, darted toward the brush.

There were no workmen around and apparently the trailer was empty as no one came out to greet them. Behind the area where the earth clearing had begun were thick woods.

Troy followed just behind Brianna as she walked around. The sun glimmered on her long blond hair, and Troy's palms itched with the desire to stroke it, to feel it cascade through his fingertips. Brunette. His fantasy woman was definitely a brunette, he told himself.

He had no idea why she'd wanted to come here, what she thought she might find, but he had a feeling she'd hoped it would be her father, maybe tied to one of the bulldozers or held captive in the trailer.

As if to confirm his thought, she walked to the trailer and stepped up to the door. She peered into the window and he saw her shoulders slump forward, indicating there was nobody there.

From the front window she moved to the other windows, looking into each one. She finally turned to face Troy, her face pale with disappointment as she walked back to where he stood. "I thought maybe…" She let her voice trail off.

"I know," he replied softly. She had a face that shouldn't know such profound sadness. Her features were made for laughter, not for grief.

"Come on, let's head out. We'll stop by your house so you can get some things, then we'll head back to the safe house."

They had only taken a couple of steps toward the car when the shot rang out and the ground next to Brianna's feet kicked up in a puff of dust.

Troy saw her eyes widen just before he threw himself at her while reaching for the gun in his ankle holster at the same time.

FOR THE SECOND TIME in a week, Brianna found herself on the ground with a hard male body over hers. Somebody had shot at her. The words screamed through her mind at the same time she realized Troy had a gun in his hand.

"It came from the woods," he whispered to her, his eyes narrowed to dangerous slits of gray ice. A fine sheen of perspiration covered his forehead as he remained unmoving for several agonizing moments.

"On the count of three, I want you to run behind that bulldozer blade." He indicated the piece of equipment nearby.

She wanted to scream that she wasn't moving anywhere, that her body was frozen with such fear, any mobility at all seemed impossible. But she also knew that having the bulldozer blade between her and the woods would be far safer than where they were now.

"Okay," she murmured, the single word shaking out of her.

"One…" His voice whispered in her ear, and every muscle she possessed tensed. "Two. Three!" He rolled off her and began to fire his weapon toward the area where the shot had come from.

A scream escaped her as she ran for the cover of the bulldozer blade, grateful when Troy made it there, as well.

She felt as if she were having a heart attack. Her chest ached with the pounding of her heart, and drawing a breath seemed nearly impossible.

Somebody had shot at her! The words bounced in her head over and over again. Why? Why would anyone want to hurt her? None of this made sense.

She nearly plastered herself against the blade, which smelled of oil and dirt, reassured by the solid metal that protected them.

Troy held his gun ready. He sat next to her, his back against the blade. She felt a trickle of perspiration trek down her back and knew it wasn't from the heat but rather from the situation.

Minutes ticked by, agonizing minutes that made her want to scream. "You think he's still there?" she finally asked, appalled to hear her voice sound so shrill.

"I don't know." He leaned out to peek around the blade. Brianna screamed as the ping of a bullet hitting the blade resounded.

"He's still there," Troy said, edging behind the protection of the thick metal.

"What happens now?" she whispered. She wanted to grab his arm, cling to him to assure herself that everything was going to be all right, but she didn't want to distract him.

"We need to call the police," she whispered.

He grimaced. "My cell phone is in the car."

Once again the minutes ticked by. Brianna closed her eyes, wondering why this was happening. Who was out there in the woods with a gun?

She wished they were back in her father's office and Troy's arms were wrapped around her like they were briefly the night before. For just those few moments she'd felt so safe, so protected.

"What do we do now?" she asked.

"We wait," he replied.

"Wait for what?" Once again her voice sounded high-pitched to her own ears.

"Wait to see what the shooter does next. Unfortunately, we're in a defensive position here and we can only react to his actions."

The sheen of perspiration had become more pronounced across his forehead and his jaw knotted with intense concentration. Brianna felt as if she was about to jump out of her skin.

She wasn't sure how much time had passed when a truck came roaring down the road and turned in to the site area. Two people got out of the truck, and Brianna was ridiculously pleased to see their familiar faces. "That's Mike Kidwell and Sandy Cartwright.

They work for me at Precious Pets," she said. "Get down!" she screamed at them.

They remained in place, perfect targets for anyone who might want to take a shot. "What's going on?" Mike shouted. "We heard gunshots."

"Bree, are you all right?" Sandy asked.

"I think the shooter is gone now," Troy said. "But I want you to get up and walk in front of me to your car."

She realized he meant to keep his body between her and any potential danger. She might think him a judgmental jerk but at the moment he definitely felt like her very own hero.

Together they got up, with him keeping her firmly against his chest as they walked toward Mike and Sandy standing at her vehicle.

She'd expected a volley of more bullets, so she breathed a small sigh of relief as they reached the car and he opened the door and pushed her into the passenger seat. Only then did he turn to introduce himself to Sandy and Mike.

"We heard the gunfire and came over to see what was going on," Mike explained, his average features twisted with worry. "There's been so much trouble here lately. I called the cops. They should be here shortly."

Sandy came to the passenger side of the car, her youthful face radiating concern. "Are you sure you're okay?" she asked worriedly. Sandy was twenty-three years old and had worked for Precious Pets as a receptionist for the past three years.

"I'm fine," Brianna assured her. She couldn't help but notice that the young woman had straightened and lightened her brown hair and now wore it like Brianna's. "I like your new hairstyle." Shock—it had to be shock that had her focusing on a hairstyle rather than the fact that somebody had shot at them.

Sandy blushed with obvious pleasure. "I thought it would be fun, you know, for Saturday. There's going to be a lot of press around that day."

"And hopefully plenty of people who want to adopt," Brianna replied as Troy got into the car.

She leaned over Troy to speak to Mike, who stood near the driver's door. "Everything in place for Saturday?" she asked.

Focus on the adoption day. Focus on the mundane, she told herself. Don't think about what just happened. God, her legs were shaking, she felt as if she might throw up and she was talking about new hairstyles and dog adoptions.

"Nothing to worry about," he assured her. "Everything is under control. Besides, I'd say you have more to worry about with what just happened."

"And we're getting out of here right now," Troy said as he started the engine with a roar. "We aren't waiting impatiently around for the police. I'm getting her out of here now. Everything is not under control," he said tersely as he peeled out of the site and back onto the road.

"Maybe not, but I've got to tell you, the gun in the ankle holster thing? Very James Bond."

He braked the car, squealing to a halt in the center of the road, and turned to stare at her incredulously. "I'm so glad you can find humor in the fact that somebody just tried to kill you."

Unexpected tears instantly burned her eyes at the sharpness of his tone. "I was trying not to think about it," she exclaimed. "Because if I think about it, I might scream."

He stared at her for a long moment, then his gaze softened. "Okay, I get it. For God's sake, don't cry."

"I'm not," she replied and quickly swiped her eyes with the back of her hands.

He took off again and for a few moments they rode in silence. "I don't understand it," she finally said. "They have my father. Why would somebody take a shot at me? What do I have to do with anything?"

Troy's knuckles were white as he gripped the steering wheel. "I think what we have to consider is that none of this is about the mall development. None of this is about your father." He turned and looked at her, his eyes piercing through her. "What we have to consider is that it's all about you."

Chapter Five

By the time they reached the Waverly house Troy was inwardly cursing himself. Had he been so captivated by the sight of the sun dancing in Brianna's pale blond hair, by the tight tug of her T-shirt across her breasts, that he hadn't paid attention to the road behind them?

Had the shooter followed them to the job site, then parked and taken a position in the woods? Dammit, Troy should have been paying less attention to his sexy companion and more attention to his job of protecting her.

He stood on the porch with Micah as Brianna ran inside the Waverly house to pack a suitcase. He'd just finished telling Micah about what had happened. "None of this is fitting together," he said to his partner with a frown. "With Brandon kidnapped, I didn't really think Brianna was in any danger. If this is about the mall, why would anyone need to hurt her if they already have Brandon?"

"You're right. And it doesn't make sense that we haven't heard anything more from whoever has Brandon," Micah replied. "But I can tell you about James Stafford. He's a community activist, a nasty fellow who has been arrested dozens of times for trespassing and a variety of other misdemeanors."

"A misdemeanor does not a kidnapper make," Troy said dryly.

"No, but according to my research he's gotten more daring the last couple of years. Last year he was a person of interest in the death of a man who owned a fur store. Unfortunately there wasn't enough evidence to arrest him, and the murder went unsolved."

This information certainly didn't put Troy's mind to rest. "I'm calling Kincaid as soon as we get to the safe house. I don't care what Heather or Brianna say about it. It's time to call in the cops."

Micah nodded in agreement. "You're right. It is time to call in some reinforcements."

"How's Heather holding up?"

"I think she's swallowing tranquilizers by the handful. She's spent most of the time I've been here in her room."

At that moment Brianna came outside, carrying both a suitcase and a computer case. Troy took the suitcase from her. "This is Dad's laptop," she said. "Maybe it will have some answers."

It was obvious to Troy that she was still focused on this being about her father and his business, despite the fact that he'd mentioned just moments before that it was possibly about her.

When they arrived back at the safe house, the first thing Brianna wanted to do was take a shower and change her clothes.

As she disappeared into the bathroom and Troy heard the sound of the water in the bath, he put in a call to the chief of police, Wendall Kincaid.

The relationship between Kincaid and the three men of Recovery Inc. had initially been contentious, but after Micah was accused of murder and Kincaid had worked with them to clear his name, the relationship had become one of cautious friendship.

Troy knew he was about to test that friendship by telling Kincaid that the kidnapping had occurred the day before but they were just now contacting him.

Troy hadn't told Brianna he was going to call and he certainly hadn't checked with Heather about his plan. No matter what the two women said, Troy knew it had to be done.

Just as he'd suspected, Kincaid was livid that they'd waited so long to contact him. "I'm beginning to think that wherever the three of you go, trouble definitely follows," he exclaimed.

Troy explained about the threats the kidnapper had made to Heather and the letter Brandon had received from James Stafford, then went on to tell him what had happened at the job site earlier that morning. "I have Brianna in a safe place."

"And I don't suppose you're willing to tell me where that might be," Wendall said dryly.

"That would be a negative," Troy replied.

"Okay, I'll get a team on this right away," Kincaid replied. "Tell Ms. Waverly that we'll do everything in our power to make sure the kidnapper doesn't know that we're working on this. The first place we'll start is with James Stafford. We're all familiar with his terrorist-type tactics."

They ended the call just as Brianna came into the kitchen. Once again she was wearing jeans and a T-shirt, this one in a bright pink that advertised Precious Pets. She brought with her the scent of sweet shampoo and the exotic fragrance of her perfume.

Troy's stomach instantly knotted with a stir of desire. It irritated him that he found her so damned attractive.

"I just called the chief of police," he said, figuring that would make her angry since he hadn't asked her permission.

"I'm glad," she said, surprising him. "It's obvious we can't find Dad. Maybe they'll be able to." Her blue eyes deepened in hue. "I just hope they're low-key enough that the kidnapper doesn't follow through on the threats he made to Heather."

She released a tremulous sigh and reached up to tuck a damp strand of hair behind her ear. "Do you think he's already dead?" The words came slowly, as if pulled from a dark and horrified place inside her.

He struggled with what to say. On the one hand, every minute that passed made it more likely that Brandon was dead. On the other hand, he couldn't possibly be the one to destroy any hope she might be harboring.

"No," he finally said. "No, I think he's still alive. We just have to find him."

To his surprise she moved toward him and he saw her need to be held, her need to connect to somebody warm and alive. And he wanted to have her in his arms so badly. He knew it was a mistake, knew he should step back, stop her forward movement. But instead, he opened his arms to her, unable to stop himself even though he knew any physical contact with her wasn't smart.

She molded herself to him and curled her arms around his neck, dizzying him with the warmth of her body and her delicious scent. He could feel her breath on his lower jaw, knew that if he dipped his head just a bit he could answer the question of what her lips would taste like.

He must be a jerk, he thought, for she was seeking comfort and he was responding with lust. It might not be his finest moment, but it was one he wouldn't trade for the world.

She didn't cry, and as her fingers touched the nape of his neck in a caress, every muscle in his body tensed. "Troy?" She softly spoke his name, and when he looked at her and saw her parted lips so close to his own, he knew he was going to kiss her.

He meant it to be a kind of toss-away kiss, a mere pecking of lips that promised nothing and delivered less. But the minute his mouth touched hers, that intention flew out of the window.

Soft and hot.

That was his first thought when their lips met. Her lips were so soft, her mouth so hot, that the idea of anything quick and light instantly fled his mind.

She opened to him, her tongue touching his as her fingers dug into the top of his shoulders. He was lost, lost in the simmering desire he'd had for her since he'd first seen her in that little black dress, lost to the surge of want that flamed through his veins.

His hands moved down her back and halted just below her waist where he could feel the slight flare of her hips. She pressed closer against him, and he knew there was no way she couldn't tell that he was aroused.

Her hands moved up once again to caress the back of his neck, and still the kiss continued, increasing his hunger for more.

He might not like the way she lived her life and he might think her values were skewed. But he loved how kissing her made the blood pound in his head, how the molded length of her against him made him not care what choices she made in her life.

He wanted to lower her to the floor, tear the T-shirt off her body and feel her warm breasts against his bare chest. He wanted to get them both naked and take her right here, right now, with no thought of consequences.

Someplace in the part of his mind that was still working he recognized that if her father was found alive, then within two weeks she'd be back to her life in California. He also recognized that as much as he knew she wasn't the woman of his dreams, she'd made it clear that he wasn't the man of her dreams, either.

If they did have sex it would be just that, hot, panting, physical need quenched without strings, without regrets.

A tinkling of music pulled him out of the moment. She dropped her hands from around his neck and sprang back from him as if he were imitation leather instead of the real thing.

"That's my cell phone," she said. Her lips were slightly swollen and her eyes held the glaze of a woman just surfacing from a trance.

"Then you'd better answer it," he said, pleased that his voice displayed none of the tension that raged through his body.

He watched the sway of her hips as she walked over to the table and didn't know whether to curse or bless the interruption.

She checked the caller ID display, then flipped open and answered. "Kent, hi. I've been meaning to call you." She drifted out of the kitchen and down the hallway toward the bedrooms.

Troy stared after her, several questions racing through his head. What might have happened if the phone hadn't rung? Would a cold shower really make him forget how much he wanted her?

And who in the hell was Kent?

BRIANNA DIDN'T KNOW what had been more startling, the fact that somebody had taken a shot at her that morning or that Troy Sinclair kissed better than any man she'd ever kissed in her life.

As she walked down the hallway toward the bedroom where she was staying, she tried to concentrate on the call and not on what had just happened in the kitchen.

Kent Goodwell had been Brianna's boyfriend through high school and until she'd left Kansas City for California. They always got together when she was in town for a visit, although it was no longer a love connection but rather a deep friendship.

"I haven't been able to call," she said into the phone as she sat on the edge of her bed. "Things have been crazy since I got here."

"You okay? You sound stressed," Kent replied.

How well he knew her. "Oh, you know, the thing on Saturday has me a little frazzled. You are coming, aren't you?"

"You know I wouldn't miss it."

"And you're adopting a dog?"

He laughed. "You know better than that. I can't

even keep my plants alive. Are you free for dinner tonight? We've got some major catching up to do."

"Can't. I'm swamped, Kent. Maybe after Saturday." She hoped, prayed that her father would be home safely by then and this whole crazy ordeal would be nothing more than a bad memory.

"Why don't you call me if you get some free time. You know I'll meet you anywhere at anytime."

She smiled with a touch of bittersweetness into the receiver. Sometimes during lonely nights in California, she regretted that Kent would always be a boy she loved, but he'd never be the man to possess her heart.

She and Kent ended the call, and she remained seated on the bed, wondering why she hadn't told him about her father's kidnapping. It just hadn't felt right to confide in him at the moment.

Kent had been a great boyfriend for a while, but they never had the kind of magic Brianna wanted when she truly fell in love. She rubbed her lower lip and tried not to remember the magic she'd felt when Troy had kissed her.

Brianna considered staying in her bedroom, but her dad's laptop was in the kitchen, and one of her goals today was to look at all his files, check his e-mail and see if anything there rang a bell of alarm.

Besides, just because she and Troy had shared a soul-stirring kiss didn't mean she intended to avoid him. It had just been a kiss, no big deal.

She returned to the kitchen where Troy was seated

at the table and staring out the window. "That was Kent Goodwell, a high school friend of mine. We usually get together whenever I'm in town, but I told him that I was too busy to meet him for lunch right now."

She knew trouble was brewing the moment she gazed into Troy's eyes. It was like looking into the center of a Midwestern storm. "Look, about what just happened," he began. "I just want you to understand that I'm very physically attracted to you, but you aren't my type at all."

She forced a small laugh to hide the stupid tinge of hurt at his words. "What are you worried about? That your kiss will make me fall head over heels in love with you and everything will get messy? I don't do messy, Troy, and besides, you've made it more than clear from the moment you met me at Dad's place that you don't like me."

"It's not that I don't like you," he quickly back-tracked. "It's just that I know the exact kind of woman I want in my life."

"Really?" She sat across the table from him. "Tell me about this paragon of womanhood."

He scowled and his eyes turned a flat metal gray. "You're making fun of me."

"No," she quickly protested. "No, I promise I'm not. I'm truly curious." Brianna didn't have a clue what kind of man would eventually capture her heart, and it intrigued her that Troy seemed to have such a clear idea of exactly what he wanted in a woman.

Besides, she didn't want to dwell on the fact that they were no closer to finding her father, didn't want to think about those bullets at the job site. Listening to Troy extol the virtues of a woman he hadn't met was safer, less emotionally draining than all the other things whirling around inside her head.

"She'll be quiet and reserved," he began.

"That definitely leaves me out," she quipped.

He scowled once again and then continued. "She'll be a simple woman who likes simple things, a woman who thinks of others before herself. She'll be a teacher or maybe a social worker, and she'll want a quiet life filled with family." He stared out the window, and for a moment the soft expression in his eyes made Brianna wish she was that woman.

And just that quickly Brianna was angry—with him, with the situation and most of all with herself for thinking such a ridiculous thought. The kind of woman he had described couldn't be further away from who she was, not that she cared.

"My father is missing, and we're sitting here talking about your love life," she said with exasperation. She grabbed her father's laptop and opened it, then punched the power button. "While you think about the love of your life, I'm going to see if I can find something on here that might give us a clue about who took my father."

If only she could take back that kiss, she thought moments later as she began to search through her father's files. If only the memory of Troy's lips on hers wasn't seared into her brain.

For those few minutes when she'd been in his arms, when his mouth had taken complete possession of hers, she'd felt like the most important woman in his world.

The afternoon passed quickly as Brianna lost herself in the computer files. At least she felt as if she were doing something constructive.

It was just after five when she stopped, and they ate a meal of sandwiches and chips. "I can't believe how many jobs my dad has going on at the same time," she said as she moved a potato chip from one side of her plate to the other. She wasn't really hungry. She was discouraged.

"Your dad is one of the most successful developers and builders in the Midwest," Troy said.

She sighed. "Yeah, but now I wonder if this is about the mall project or maybe something else he was working on."

"But we know for sure the mall development was the one your father was worried about, the one that has been the most volatile," Troy reminded her.

She stared out the window, where twilight had begun to tie deep purple shadows around the base of the trees and in the low-lying brush. And following twilight would be night—another night without her knowing if she'd ever see her father again, another night of not knowing if he was dead or alive.

"You aren't eating," Troy said. Those gray eyes of his seemed to be looking deep inside her.

She stared down at the sandwich on her plate, her appetite banished by the fear that lingered deep inside her. Refusing to show him her fear, not wanting even to acknowledge it herself, she cast him a sassy smile.

"It's not exactly up to my usual standards," she said airily and got up from the table. She carried her plate to the trash can and dumped the contents, then placed the dish in the sink.

She was acutely aware of Troy watching her and knew her smart remark had probably irritated him. But that was okay with her. She had a feeling the more distance she kept from Troy Sinclair, the better.

After dinner Brianna returned to her father's laptop, and Troy went into the living room to watch television. Once again she found herself staring out the window, where the night had deepened and the loneliness that had plagued her for the last couple of months in California returned.

Oh, she'd had a couple of boyfriends in the last few years, but neither of them had been bring-home-to-dad material. Both had been good-time guys who enjoyed having her on her arm in public, but seemed less interested in her when they were alone.

She was a living cliché, a rich girl who lived a public life but found herself alone in bed most nights wondering what it would be like to have somebody she cared about next to her.

By nine o'clock she felt as if her eyes were crossing with all the files she'd read on the computer. She got up from the table and stretched her arms over her head, then froze as she heard the familiar sound of Troy's cell phone ringing from the living room.

She raced into the living room where he was seated on the sofa. As he pulled the phone from his pocket, every nerve in her body went on alert, and adrenaline flooded her veins in such strength that she felt half-nauseous.

Had the kidnapper called? Was there finally a ransom call? It was impossible to tell from Troy's end of the conversation who was on the other end of the line. He stood and paced the room while he listened to the caller.

When he finally hung up, she was at his side. "Was that Lucas or Micah? Has something happened?" She grabbed his forearm and prayed for good news.

He shook his head. "That was Wendall Kincaid. He called to give me an update on what the authorities are doing. They've got a tail on James Stafford, but so far he's done nothing suspicious. They've put a trace and trap on the phone line at your house, so they'll quickly be able to identify the location of any call that comes in. They've also got some men watching the house."

"But won't the kidnapper know? Won't he see

that there are cops everywhere?" She tightened her grip on his arm, remembering the threat that the kidnapper had made when he'd called Heather.

Troy placed a hand over hers. "He'll never see them. Trust me, Wendall knows what the stakes are, and he doesn't want a mistake to be made, either."

Some of the tension left her but she didn't move away from him. She liked the feel of his strong arm beneath her fingertips, the warmth that radiated from his body with the promise to heat the cold places inside her.

She stared into his eyes and saw a flash of something dark, something delicious—a want, a hunger. She wanted to fall into it, fall into him. It didn't matter that she wasn't the kind of woman he wanted for the rest of his life. It only mattered that she be the woman he wanted for the rest of this night.

A new tension rocked through her, and she moved her hand from his arm to his chest where she could feel the rapid beat of his heart.

"What are you doing, Brianna?" His voice was low, with a hint of danger in it.

"I don't know," she admitted, fighting against a shiver of pleasure at his scent, his very nearness.

Anticipation sparked in the air and she leaned closer to him, wanting to lose herself in him.

He took her by the shoulders and gently pushed her back. "I'm not one of your Hollywood boy toys, Bree. When I take a woman to bed it means something, and we both know that if we fall into bed together tonight it will mean nothing." He dropped his hands to his sides. "I'm going to my room. I'll see you in the morning."

She watched him walk down the hallway, and for just a moment she wished she were a simple woman with simple needs. Or at least that Troy Sinclair wasn't such an honorable man.

Chapter Six

"I want to go to the meeting tonight," Brianna said the next morning as she and Troy sat at the kitchen table drinking coffee.

"Have you lost your mind?" he replied. He'd gotten up on the wrong side of the bed that morning, having spent the night before dreaming about wild, hot sex with Brianna. "Have you forgotten that somebody tried to shoot you yesterday?"

"Of course I haven't forgotten," she replied with that easy flippancy that simply increased his ire. "But last night I found some notes Dad had made for the meeting, and I think I should be there in his place. Besides, yesterday we were out in the middle of nowhere. The meeting is in a community center and there will be plenty of people around. Nobody is going to hurt me with witnesses everywhere."

She smiled, that ridiculously charming grin that made him want to grin back at her. "Besides," she said, "I have complete and total faith in you as my bodyguard. My father wouldn't hire anyone second-rate."

"I can be your bodyguard, but I'm not a super-hero," he replied grudgingly.

"I just think it's important that I be there," she replied, all the humor gone from her pretty blue eyes. "Maybe we'll see or hear something that will turn into a lead. And if nothing else, I need to be there to show those people that Waverlys don't quit, that we won't be bullied by threats."

He leaned back in his chair and fought the impulse to raise a hand to his forehead, where a dull ache had begun to throb. This was so not what he'd signed up for. It was supposed to have been an easy job, a couple of days of babysitting a woman he'd known he wouldn't like.

He hadn't counted on Brandon Waverly being kidnapped, hadn't figured on there being a real threat against Brianna and he sure as hell hadn't been prepared to want her, to find himself actually liking her.

"Brianna, I just don't think it's a good idea," he said.

"Thank you for your opinion but I'm still going to that meeting."

She had that look in her eyes, the same one she'd had when he'd left her at the Waverly house and she'd said she wasn't going anywhere but had snuck out after dark.

He knew that if he didn't agree to take her, somehow, someway she'd figure out how to get to that community center under her own steam. She was smart and resourceful and as stubborn as a mule.

"Okay, then I guess we're going to the meeting," he relented, his mind already racing with all the things that could go wrong.

"Don't look so worried," she replied, that warm smile curving her lips once again. "It's not like I have a death wish. I just don't think I'll be in any danger."

"You realize you're taking a risk."

Her smile faltered. "I know, but I think the risk is small compared to the potential of maybe learning something that might help find my father."

Troy found it difficult to argue with her need to do something, anything to help find Brandon. If one of his family members had been kidnapped, he'd try to move heaven and earth to find them.

"How about I make breakfast this morning?" she offered.

He raised an eyebrow. "Can you do that?"

She laughed and the pleasant sound warmed him. "You'd be surprised what I can do when I set my mind to it."

A few minutes later he watched as she bustled around the kitchen, gathering the ingredients for omelets. He reminded himself that this woman in her jeans and T-shirt, wearing little makeup and preparing to cook breakfast, wasn't the real Bree Waverly.

She was obviously trying to make the best of a bad situation, but when this was all over she'd go back to California, she'd be back in the tabloids and living a lifestyle he didn't even want to understand.

It was the kind of lifestyle Holly had wanted but had been afraid he wouldn't be able to provide when the rumors had started about his family wealth taking a hit in the stock market. He shoved away thoughts of the young woman who had broken his heart so long ago.

Breakfast was pleasant, and as they ate, they talked a little bit about their childhoods. Troy had grown up in a loving environment with his parents and three older sisters.

"They tormented me to death," he exclaimed. "I had long hair when I was younger, and they'd practice hairstyles on me."

Brianna laughed. "I can just see you as a little boy with blond curls and bright pink ribbons in your hair."

"I'm surprised I'm not scarred by the experience," he replied with a grin.

"Are you close to them now?" she asked.

"Very. They're all married and have kids, but we're all really close."

"You want kids?"

He nodded. "Someday, sure. I definitely want a family. What about you?"

"Definitely kids, at least two. I always wished my mom and dad would have had a chance to give me either an older or a younger sibling. Growing up as an only child can be so lonely."

"There were times I wished I were an only child," he replied with a grin.

She smiled. "And you have your friendships with Lucas and Micah. Must be nice," she said with a touch of wistfulness. "Growing up it was just me and my dad, and I didn't have many friends."

"But surely you have lots of friends in California," he replied.

She frowned. "I have party friends, people who like to be seen with me, who hope their picture will be taken with me. I have people who use me to get invited to a party, or who want to hang out because I'm Bree. To be honest, I'd hate to have to depend on any of them for anything."

She laughed and waved a hand as if to dismiss her words. "I was sitting here last night and thinking that I'm the cliché of the poor little rich girl who has no friends. I don't trust that the people around me have my best interests at heart. I've learned to be cautious about relationships."

Troy understood what she was saying. There were many positives about being wealthy, but that was one of the negatives—the fear that whoever entered your life did so because of money and not because of you. The fear was very real because the possibility was very real.

"You're probably thinking I'm being a whiny brat," she continued.

"No, not at all. I know exactly what you're talking

about." He hesitated a moment, old memories nudging him. "There was a woman when I was young, before I joined the service. I thought I was in love with her and I thought she loved me, too. I asked her to marry me and she said yes, and I started to plan our future together."

It had been one of the most painful experiences of his life, but he was surprised that the memory no longer hurt, that either enough time had passed or he had gained enough maturity to erase the heartache he'd felt at the time.

"I don't know who started the rumor," he continued, "but word got out that my family had lost a ton of money in a stock market deal. It wasn't true, but apparently Holly, my new fiancée, thought it was. She immediately broke off the engagement, and I realized then that she hadn't loved me, she'd loved the lifestyle she thought my money could buy for her."

"Oh, Troy, I'm so sorry for you." Brianna's eyes were dark with compassion.

He smiled. "Don't be. She actually did me a favor. Right after the breakup I joined the Navy and the rest, as they say, is history."

Even though she was nothing like the woman he eventually wanted to spend his life with, it surprised him how easy it was to talk to Brianna. There was an openness about her, a comfortable give-and-take that was far too appealing.

After breakfast Brianna returned to the task of

checking files on her father's laptop, and Troy called Lucas at the Waverly house to see if there'd been any new developments. There were none. He then called Kincaid to see what leads the authorities had, but Wendall had nothing concrete. So Troy went back to the master bedroom where he had been sleeping and where there was a computer on a desk.

He sat at the desk and powered up the computer, hoping that he could find a picture of the community center where the meeting would be held that evening.

If he were going to provide protection for Brianna against an unknown threat, he'd prefer to get a handle on the layout of the place.

Thank God for technology, he thought as he found the appropriate Web page that not only offered the prices of renting the community building, but also showed views of both the inside and outside.

He studied the pictures for a long time, memorizing the floor plans and considering options. Even though he had no reason to believe that anyone would try to hurt Brianna in the middle of a public meeting, a heavy knot of apprehension twisted in his gut.

He just had a bad feeling about the whole thing, but he knew a bad feeling wouldn't be enough to keep Brianna away.

His bad feeling still weighed him down at six-thirty that evening when they got ready to leave the house. He wore a pair of dress pants and a short-sleeved white dress shirt. Brianna was clad in a royal blue dress that thankfully wasn't as short or as sexy as the little black number she'd worn on the night he'd had dinner at the Waverly house.

"Nervous?" he asked once they were in the car and pulling out onto the highway. He checked his rear-view mirror, making sure nobody was following them. The last thing he wanted was for anyone to know where she was stashed for now.

"Not really." She clutched the file folder of notes she'd prepared. "I just want to do what Dad would have done if he'd been here, calm the crowd and assure them that the mall is a good thing."

"You think you'll be able to do that?"

"I think part of the problem is when people hear the word *mall,* they think of this huge monstrosity with thousands of parking spaces and a hundred shops. That's not what this is going to be. It was just going to be six or eight shops, and Dad was hoping to bring in a restaurant and grocer for the convenience of everyone who currently has to drive some distance to eat out or buy groceries."

She frowned and stared out the window, and Troy knew her thoughts were on her missing father. Troy tightened his grip on the steering wheel and wished there was something he could say to ease her worry, but anything he might say would be nothing more than empty platitudes. And Brianna was smart enough to recognize them for what they would be—worthless.

Troy didn't see a happy ending to any of this. The

fact that Brandon had been missing for three days with no contact from the kidnapper led him to believe that Brandon Waverly would eventually be found dead. He knew that Brianna's grief would break his heart.

The community center was located not far from the mall site. It was a small brick building, and despite the fact that they were early, Troy was surprised to see that the parking lot was already filled with cars. There was an overflow area on the opposite side of the road and he pulled in there to park.

"Now I'm a little bit nervous," she confessed. "There are more people here than I expected."

He grinned at her. "I can't believe it. Bree Waverly, one of the paparazzis' favorites, is nervous about getting up in front of a bunch of people?"

"Bree isn't here at the moment. It's just me, plain old Brianna," she replied. "And all I want to do is make things better for when my dad gets back home."

If her dad got back, Troy thought as he got out of the car and came around to the passenger side. As she stood, he immediately wrapped an arm around her as his gaze shot from side to side, seeking any potential threats.

He hurried her toward the building, breathing a bit easier when they got through the front doors. Just inside an off-duty police officer greeted them.

He introduced himself as Ben Tremain. He'd been

hired by Brandon the week before to attend the meeting in case there were problems. His presence went a long way in easing some of Troy's concerns. Surely Brianna would be safe here with ordinary people surrounding them and a police officer as well as Troy watching over her.

The community center consisted of two rooms, the large meeting space and a smaller kitchen area. Chairs were arranged theater-style facing a wooden podium, and behind the podium were a couple of chairs. Troy led her there, away from the crowd milling about at the back of the room.

They sat side by side and watched as more people arrived. "You see anybody you know?" he asked. He was tense, on edge and ready to respond to anyone who tried to get too close to her.

His tension grew as he saw a tall, dark-haired man enter the room. James Stafford. Troy recognized him because he'd done a little research into the community activist that afternoon on the Internet.

Stafford was dressed in a business suit, but the nice fit and expensive material didn't take away from his thuglike appearance. He carried himself with an arrogant swagger and greeted most of the people in the room by their first names.

When he started toward the front of the room where Troy and Brianna were seated, Troy stood and took several steps forward, presenting himself as a barrier between the man and Brianna.

"And you are?" Stafford asked, meeting Troy's gaze with a hint of challenge.

"Troy Sinclair, and I know who you are, Mr. Stafford."

James flashed a grin that displayed a chipped front tooth. "I'm the man who is going to shut down this operation." He looked over Troy's shoulder to Brianna. "Where's your daddy, girl? He afraid to show his face to these good people?"

Troy narrowed his eyes. "Why don't you take a seat, Mr. Stafford. The meeting is going to begin in just a few minutes."

Troy held James's stare for a long moment, then the big man stepped back and took a seat in the front row. Troy returned to the chair next to Brianna's.

"That's James Stafford," he whispered to her.

"He asked why Dad isn't here. I guess he doesn't have anything to do with the kidnapping."

Either that or the man was cunning, Troy thought. It looked like it was going to be a tough crowd. No smiles were cast in their direction, and even though it was crazy, Troy felt himself nervous on Brianna's behalf.

It was as if James Stafford sitting down was a signal for the rest of the group to take their seats. Once everyone had found a chair, silence descended and Brianna stood.

A little bit of Troy's tension eased as he perused the group. Mostly it was gray-haired men in overalls with white-haired women at their sides. The only person who looked half-dangerous was James Stafford, and Troy intended to watch the man carefully.

"Good evening," Brianna began. "For those of you who don't know me, I'm Brandon Waverly's daughter, Brianna." If she was nervous her voice didn't betray it. She spoke loud and strong, without a single quiver.

"Where's your father?" James called from his front row seat. "Is he afraid to be here and face these good people?" Several people raised their voices in support of Stafford.

Brianna held up a hand. "My father couldn't be here tonight, but I'm here to discuss your concerns and answer any questions you might have."

And for the next two hours, that's what she did. As she told them about the mall her father had envisioned, Troy thought of the conversation they'd shared that afternoon.

She'd told him that she was a cliché of the poor little rich girl, but he had made her a cliché in the way he had stereotyped her without knowing much of anything about her.

He'd had her pegged as shallow, as a shopping, partying machine who cared about little else. He'd been wrong.

She was far more complicated a woman than he'd initially thought. Devoted to her father, brave to the point of near recklessness, she touched something in him, something more than sharp, hot desire.

As she continued to talk, he sensed the mood of the crowd changing, and he realized she was slowly winning them over.

"I just don't see why we need a restaurant around here," one old man exclaimed.

"Wouldn't you enjoy going someplace where you can get a nice slice of roast beef or a piece of apple pie?" Brianna asked him.

"I can stay home and get that," he replied and looked at the woman next to him. "Emma here makes the finest apple pie in the county."

"But maybe Emma is tired of making pies. Maybe she'd like to be taken out someplace where she can just sit and relax and somebody else waits on her," Brianna countered.

"You got that right," Emma quipped and then blushed.

Everyone laughed and Brianna grinned. "I'll tell you what—when the restaurant is complete, I'll make sure you two have a lovely dinner on me."

"You can't bribe these people to make it right," Stafford exclaimed and jumped to his feet.

"Yes, she can," somebody yelled from the back, and again the room erupted in laughter.

Stafford returned to his seat, his dark eyes narrowed in disgust. He obviously wasn't happy with the tone the meeting had taken.

Troy wondered if the community activist had hidden Brandon away someplace. Had the kidnapping been so that Brandon couldn't make this meeting and so that the tension between the people and the builder would increase?

If that were the case, was it possible that Brandon would be released in the morning? Was Stafford a man who would resort to murder as a means to an end? Time would tell.

It was after nine and darkness had fallen when the meeting finally drew to an end. Troy was surprised to realize that he was proud of Brianna, proud of how she'd handled the crowd, of the intelligent answers she'd given.

She'd gone a long way in waylaying the fears that somehow the mall would bring in criminal elements and trouble. Instead she'd made the people see the benefits the small mall would bring to the area.

Troy remained seated next to her as the crowd dispersed. He didn't want her mingling, hadn't forgotten that somebody had tried to stab her in the middle of a crowd in California.

When there was nobody left inside except Ben, Troy and Brianna stood to leave. "You did a great job, Ms. Waverly," Ben said as the three walked to the door.

"Thanks. I think it went pretty well," she replied. Her cheeks were flushed with color and her eyes sparkled with a winner's confidence. She'd never looked so lovely.

"Good night now," Ben said at the door.

"Good night," they replied and stepped out into the balmy night air.

The parking lot was empty except for one car, and as they started across the property to the overflow lot across the highway, James Stafford stepped out of the building shadows.

"You win this round, Ms. Waverly, but don't think you've won the war."

Troy stepped closer to Brianna as he heard the ugly tone in Stafford's voice. He didn't like the fact that the man had waited until everyone had left to confront them.

"We aren't at war," Brianna replied coolly. "It's called progress, Mr. Stafford. Eventually retail shops are going to come to that area of the city. It's inevitable. The city is expanding northward at a rapid rate. These people can either deal with my father, who is trying to be sensitive to their needs, or they can deal with another developer who simply won't care what feathers he ruffles."

She continued to impress Troy with her intelligence, with the way she met Stafford's glare directly. She looked like a lean, dainty warrior.

"I'm not concerned about years from now. I'm worried about right now," Stafford replied, his gaze narrowed with menace.

"I think, Mr. Stafford, that what you like is publicity and getting your name and picture in the papers," Brianna replied.

The big man snorted. "Takes one to know one," he replied.

"I'm done here," she said and started toward the far parking lot.

As Stafford started after her, Troy stepped in front of the man. "I wouldn't do that," he said in a low, calm voice. "In fact, if I were you I'd make sure I stay as far away from Brianna Waverly as I possibly could." For all Troy knew, this was the man who had kidnapped Brandon and was holding him some-place…or worse.

Before Stafford could reply, the air filled with the sound of a revving engine and the sudden squeal of tires. Troy turned and looked toward the highway. His blood iced, freezing him in place for a moment, as a car appeared out of nowhere and raced toward Brianna, who stood frozen in the center of the road like a deer caught in bright headlights.

"Brianna!" he screamed.

The car didn't swerve or slow down as it roared toward her, and then it was gone—and so was she.

Chapter Seven

Brianna careened down an embankment, crying out as her body slammed against rocks and debris. She thought she was going to fall forever, but she finally came to a stop, her heart pounding painfully fast.

She didn't move, was afraid that any movement would hurt. Had she broken bones? She was scared to find out.

The stars overhead winked down at her as she remained on her back. If she hadn't jumped when she had, she'd be dead. Whoever had been driving that car had meant to kill her.

"Brianna!"

Troy's frantic voice split the silence of the night.

"Over here," she managed to reply.

She heard him careening down the embankment, and tears blurred her vision as she realized just how close death had come.

She'd felt the heat of the car, smelled the fumes as it had missed her by mere inches. The headlights had been blinding, and she'd been helplessly frozen in the glare of death.

Troy reached where she lay, and he bent down over her, his features obscured by the moonlight at his back. "Are you all right?" What she couldn't see on his face she heard in his voice—a low, rich fear.

"I don't know. I think so." She started to sit up.

"Don't move. We need to call for an ambulance," Troy said.

"No, I'm fine," she assured him. As she managed to sit up, she realized that James Stafford stood just behind Troy.

"Is she okay?" he asked as if Brianna wasn't present.

"I'm fine," she repeated, realizing she didn't seem to have any broken bones. Troy helped her to her feet, his arm firmly around her for support.

"You know I didn't have anything to do with this, right?" Stafford asked, clearly worried. "I don't work this way."

Brianna felt the tension in Troy's body as he half carried her back up to the top of the deep ditch. Stafford followed behind them. Troy led her to the car, opened the passenger seat and helped her ease inside, then he turned back to the tall activist.

"Did you see what kind of car it was?" he asked.

Stafford shook his head. "It all happened so fast and it was so dark. All I saw were the headlights and her frozen in the middle of the road."

"I'm getting her out of here," Troy said and closed her car door.

Brianna watched as the two men talked for a moment longer, then Troy slid in behind the steering wheel as Stafford walked back across the highway to where his car was parked in front of the community building.

"Are you sure you're okay?" Troy asked as he started the engine. "Maybe we should take you to the emergency room and get you checked out."

"No, that's really not necessary, although my body is starting to hurt in places I didn't know I had." She tried to offer him a smile, but it crumbled as a fierce trembling overtook her. "Just take me home, Troy."

"Just hang tight. I'll have you there in no time," he said. As they pulled onto the highway, he checked the rearview mirror, and she knew he was making sure they weren't being followed.

She leaned her head back and closed her eyes, unable to stop reliving those moments when she'd been frozen in place and the car had come out of nowhere with the apparent intent of striking her.

Her trembling increased, and despite the heat of the night, she knew it would be a long time before she felt warm again.

They didn't speak any more on the ride back to the safe house. The euphoria of the meeting, the sense of success she'd felt when it had ended, had been destroyed. All she was left with was a growing fear that she didn't want to face.

When they reached the house, Troy helped her inside and to the sofa, then he disappeared into the bathroom and she heard water running in the tub. A bath. He was fixing her a bath.

Once again she closed her eyes and imagined the hot water soothing muscles that were already screaming in pain. A hot bath was exactly what she needed and wanted, and she was vaguely surprised that Troy had recognized it.

He came out of the bathroom. "Maybe a bath will help keep you from waking up in the morning feeling like you've been hit by a truck."

"Thanks." It felt unreal. Things like this didn't happen in her life. Dear God, what was happening to her life? She tamped down a rising hysteria.

"Brianna, could you tell what kind of car it was? Maybe a color?"

She shook her head. "It was all just an awful blur." With a tremendous effort she got to her feet.

"I've got a bottle of Scotch in the kitchen if you think a shot would help."

She shook her head. "I'm not much of a drinker. I don't suppose you have any tea?"

"Sure. You want a cup of hot tea?" His forehead was creased with a furrow of worry and his buzz-cut blond hair appeared to be standing on end more than usual.

"That would be great. I like it with just a little bit

of milk and a spoonful of sugar. Could you just set it inside the bathroom door when it's ready?"

"No problem," he agreed. "Brianna, are you sure you don't need a doctor?"

"Positive. Everything is working the way it's supposed to. I'll be fine." She struggled to give him a reassuring smile.

As she walked to the bathroom, she thought how ridiculous it was that they were talking about tea-time instead of the fact that somebody had tried to kill her.

Once inside the small room, she stared at her re-flection in the floor-length mirror on the back of the bathroom door. Her dress was ruined—grass-stained and with one arm torn. Her panty hose sported runs and holes. She was a mess, but she was alive.

And somebody tried to kill you.

The words echoed in her head as she stripped. She noticed Troy had set out a fluffy towel and a bottle of bubble bath. She added some of the jasmine-scented liquid to the water, wondering how many other women had been here in the past.

Once the tub was filled with bubbles, she slid into the water with a hiss of pleasure.

Somebody tried to kill you.

She'd written off the attack in California as an isolated incident that might or might not have had anything to do with her personally. She'd even managed to dismiss the shooting at the mall job site as something that had nothing to do with her personally, but more with her father's business.

However, it was more difficult to put a positive spin on what had happened tonight. That car had been lying in wait for her. It had sat on the road, lights off and engine idling until she'd reached the center of the road. Then it had roared to life with the full intention of striking her dead.

Who was doing this? How could she protect herself from danger when she didn't know from which direction the danger came?

A soft knock sounded on the door. She checked to make sure she was submerged beneath the cover of bubbles. "You can come in, I'm bubble decent," she said.

The door opened and he stepped just inside, looking ridiculously ill at ease holding a dainty teacup and saucer and with his gaze averted toward the ceiling.

She might have found him judgmental and a bit of a jerk when she'd first met him, but at the moment, feeling more vulnerable than she ever had in her life, her heart opened to him in a way it hadn't to a man in a very long time.

"Something interesting up there?" she asked with a touch of humor.

His gaze drifted downward to meet hers and his cheeks turned a charming ruddy color. "I didn't want to invade your privacy any more than necessary," he replied.

"I'm covered."

"I can see that." His gaze swept over her, then he quickly looked away again. He set the teacup on the sink counter. "Is there anything else you need?"

"No, I'm fine. Thanks for the tea," she said, her mouth suddenly dry.

"No problem." He turned and left the room, but not before she saw the heat in his eyes, a heat that raised the temperature of the water around her.

He wanted her. She submerged herself deeper into the scented water. He might not like her. He might not like what he believed about her lifestyle, but he damn straight wanted her.

And she wanted him.

She liked him. He was not only physically strong but also possessed a quiet confidence that drew her to him. In many ways he reminded her of her father, a straight shooter who spoke his mind, a man who made his decisions based on a strong moral code and who ultimately had her best interests at heart.

He could have easily walked away from this assignment when her dad had been kidnapped. The man who was paying his fee may no longer be capable of doing that.

Her heart squeezed tightly at this particular thought. She realized she just wasn't ready to face the possibility of never seeing her father again.

Troy could have deposited her back at the Waverly house and washed his hands of the whole mess, but he hadn't done that. He was still here with her, protecting her, but her gratefulness had nothing to do with the fact that she wanted him.

She pulled herself from the bathtub and grabbed the towel that Troy had laid out for her. She dried herself and her hair, then wrapped the damp towel around her body and stood at the counter to sip the warm tea.

Troy had told her he had a specific type of woman in mind for his future, and Brianna knew she was nothing like the woman he'd eventually marry.

But he hadn't found that woman yet, and they were here together and she needed his arms around her to take away the ice that chilled her core.

She finished her tea and used the brush from the counter to work the tangles out of her hair. The bath had helped soothe some of the muscle aches and pains, but not all of them. Her roll down the embankment had torn the skin off her knee and one elbow, but considering how fast and how far she had rolled, she was grateful she hadn't broken any bones.

She opened the bathroom door and ran across the hallway and into the bedroom where she had been staying. She pulled on her nightclothes and her robe, then dropped the towel in the hamper back in the bathroom, grabbed the empty cup and saucer and went into the living room.

Troy sat on the sofa with the television playing softly. "Better?" he asked.

"Better," she agreed, "but I have a feeling I'm

going to feel like I was hit by a truck in the morning." She carried the dishes to the kitchen and put them in the dishwasher, then returned to the living room and sat next to him on the sofa.

"We need to talk," he said, his eyes deep gray and somber. "I called Wendall Kincaid and told him what happened. Unfortunately, I don't think there were any other witnesses, and James and I couldn't tell what kind of a car it was, so I doubt if Kincaid will be able to do anything about it."

"I don't want to talk about it right now." She knew he wanted to discuss what had happened, but she didn't even want to think about it, much less talk about it. "You probably don't know this about me, but denial is one of my favorite states of mind."

"There's no way we can deny what happened tonight," he replied.

Somebody tried to kill you.

The words jumped unbidden to her mind, bringing with them a chunk of ice that sat unwelcomed in her chest. She fought against a shiver.

She leaned forward and placed a hand on Troy's forearm and instantly felt his muscles tense. "Can we just maintain a state of denial for the rest of tonight?" she asked. "It's almost bedtime and I don't want to have any nightmares."

He looked at her in surprise and at the same time muted the television. "Are you prone to nightmares?"

"No, but I've never had anyone trying to run over

me with a car before." She moved closer to him and leaned her head against his shoulder. His body was still tense, but wonderfully warm. He smelled marvelous, like his distinctive cologne and, more important, like safety.

"Maybe if I slept in your bed with you tonight I'd feel better." She raised her head to look at him. The ice inside her melted just a bit beneath the intense heat in his gaze.

"I DON'T THINK that's a good idea," he said, his voice a low rumble. He knew he should scoot away from her, gain enough distance that he could breathe without smelling the clean, delicious scent of her.

"I think it's a wonderful idea," she replied and snuggled closer to him.

She had no idea what she was doing to him, couldn't know that every nerve ending he possessed was electrified by her closeness.

He'd been electrified since the moment he'd stepped into the bathroom and caught sight of her in the tub. Although most of her had been covered in bubbles, he couldn't help but notice the silkiness of her bare shoulders, the erotic length of her neck with her hair splayed back from her face.

He'd wanted nothing more than to strip naked and climb into that steaming water with her. As he'd thought about how close that car had come to hitting her, how quickly she could have been killed, he'd wanted to wrap her up in his arms and feel the steady beat of her heart against his own, assure himself that she was really alive and okay.

But there was no way he could be in a bed next to her and just want to hear her heartbeat. He'd want more. So very much more.

Even at this moment he was wondering what she was wearing beneath the short pink terry cloth robe. Did she have on a silky little nightgown or was she naked?

"I need a snuggle buddy," she replied, her breath warm against the underside of his jaw.

"I'm not good at snuggling," he replied, his throat feeling as if it were closing up.

"Oh, I think you underestimate yourself," she replied.

Her hair smelled like citrus shampoo, and he wanted to bury his fingers in it, feel those golden strands slide through his fingertips. He wanted to caress her skin and see if it was as soft as he suspected.

"Brianna, I can't sleep with you. I mean, I'm not sure I can be in a bed next to you and remain a gentleman." It was a hard thing for him to confess, that he was weak where she was concerned.

Once again she raised her face up to look at him. Her blue eyes shimmered with just enough impishness to heat his blood. "Troy, I'm desperately hoping you won't be a gentleman."

He was lost. He was unaware that he was going

to kiss her until their lips met and his hands slid up into her silky hair.

As with the first time he kissed her, he was stunned by the heat her mouth offered his and his swift reaction to it. He made an attempt to pull back, to stop from making what he knew would be a mistake, but she wound her arms more tightly around his neck and slid her tongue into his mouth.

She was temptation itself, and he was weak where she was concerned. Her body was warm and sweet-smelling, and her lips plied his with a heat that enflamed him.

The kiss seemed to last forever, stealing half his breath and making his chest hurt from the rapid pounding of his heart. When they finally broke apart, she slid out of his arms and off the sofa.

"Don't think, Troy. Tonight isn't the time for talking or for thinking. I almost died and what I want now is for you to hold me, to make me feel wonderfully alive." She held her hand out for his and he found himself reaching out and standing.

Big mistake, he told himself as they walked down the long hallway to the master bedroom. He should stop this madness at the door, send her to her own bedroom and call it a night.

But when they reached the bedroom door, she unbelted her robe and allowed it to fall from her shoulders, leaving her standing before him in a pale pink chemise and thong underpants.

At the moment he couldn't imagine his mind creating a fantasy woman he wanted more than the living, breathing woman standing in front of him.

She walked with him to the side of the bed, then molded herself to him. His arms wrapped around her, holding her so tightly he could feel the banging of her heart against his own.

Once again their lips met in a fiery kiss that not only removed any hesitation from his mind but also erased the capacity for rational thought.

As the kiss continued her fingers danced at the front of his shirt, unfastening the buttons with frantic need. When the buttons were all freed, she swept the shirt off his shoulders. As the garment fell to the ground behind him, her palms splayed against his bare skin.

He pulled his mouth from hers and looked down at her, wanting to make sure there was no doubt in her eyes, no second thoughts about what they were going to do.

From the hall light spilling into the dark bedroom he could see the glimmer in her eyes. He saw hunger there, and need, but he didn't see anything that even resembled doubt.

"I'm getting into bed," she said, her voice a husky whisper. As she turned to walk to the side of the bed, her naked buttocks were clearly visible and Troy felt as if he were about to explode.

As she got into bed, he sat on the opposite side and

removed his ankle holster and gun. He set them on the nightstand along with his cell phone. He removed a condom from his wallet, then placed it on the nightstand, as well.

He was surprised to feel a shaking in his hands, shocked to realize he felt like a teenager about to have sex for the very first time.

It took him only moments to remove his shoes and socks and take off his slacks, then he slid beneath the covers and she rolled into his arms.

Once again they kissed, tongues moving as if battling for dominance, gasps of pleasure filling the air. He caressed the length of her back, loving the feel of her skin and her soft mewls of pleasure with each touch.

Her hands worked up and down his back, lingering at the waist of his briefs, briefs that had suddenly grown painfully small.

As their kissing and caressing grew more frenzied, he kicked off his underwear at the same time she sat up and pulled the chemise over her head and then removed her thong.

They came back together completely naked, and Troy cupped her breasts in his hands and rubbed his thumbs over her nipples. She gasped with pleasure and he dipped his head to capture one of the turgid peaks in his mouth.

As he sucked and teased, she writhed beneath him, her obvious pleasure increasing his own. He moved one of his hands down the smooth flat of her abdomen, sliding lower…lower still until his fingers found her damp heat.

She moaned and moved her hips to meet his touch, and he came precariously close to losing it. But he wanted to give her pleasure before he took his own, knowing that once he entered her, things were going to be very quick, despite his wish to the contrary.

He moved his fingers against her and felt the tension building up inside her. She softly gasped his name and he loved the way it sounded on her lips. She said his name again, this time with a half laugh of pleasure as she stiffened. He felt the shudders that rippled through her, then she went limp, as if all the bones in her body had melted away.

She was still only a moment, then she reached down and encircled his hardness with her hand. He gasped with a pleasure so intense it made it difficult for him to draw breath.

Her mouth moved to the hollow of his throat, then down his chest, shooting jolts of electricity through him wherever it touched.

She was obviously not willing to be a passive taker, but rather wanted to be a giving participant in their lovemaking. Her mouth continued a downward track as she stroked him, and he realized he couldn't take it any longer, that he was precariously close to losing it.

With a strangled gasp he rolled away from her and grabbed the condom wrapper from the nightstand. It took only seconds for him to get it out and on.

She must have sensed his urgent need, for she rolled on her back and welcomed him between her thighs. Before taking her he kissed her again, a deep, searing kiss that moved him not only on a physical level, but an emotional one.

And then he could wait no longer. He entered her, hissing pleasure as she wrapped her legs around his back to draw him in deeper. He didn't move, simply savored the sensations that rippled through him. If there had been any thoughts left in his head, they vanished as he gave himself to the act of making love to her.

Slowly at first they moved together, then faster. Her hands gripped his buttocks as he rocked into her. Their gazes locked as their movements became more frenzied.

He wanted to last forever, to keep that glaze of bliss in her eyes, but all too quickly he felt himself building, and with a hoarse cry he reached his release. He collapsed with his upper body just off hers and drew in a lungful of air.

Her fingers waltzed up his back and she released a sigh of contentment. "You're a fantastic snuggle buddy," she whispered.

A small burst of laughter left him. "You make it remarkably easy." He disengaged from her and rolled off the side of the bed. "I'll be right back," he said and headed for the small adjoining bathroom.

A few moments later he stood in front of the

mirror and stared at his reflection. What are you doing, man? He'd been conflicted about his feelings for her before, and making love with her had only made things worse.

She had a life in California and he'd be a fool to get hung up on her, a fool to believe that he could ever be enough for a woman like Brianna, not that he'd even want to be.

She was complicated, and he wanted simple. She was demanding and spoiled, and he wanted sweet self-lessness. He closed his eyes and tried to summon the picture of his fantasy woman. It worried him that the only vision that entered his mind was one of Brianna.

Chapter Eight

Brianna awoke slowly, coming to consciousness with a sense of well-being she'd never felt in her life. Troy.

He was her first conscious thought and she reached a hand out only to discover that she was alone in his bed.

When she opened her eyes and saw the sunshine streaming through the window, she realized he'd probably gotten up some time ago.

She rolled to his side of the bed and buried her head in his pillow, capturing the faint lingering scent of him. She had no illusions about what they'd done the night before. It had been a combination of vulnerability and lust that had driven her into his bed, but she wouldn't take back a minute of it.

As she hugged his pillow close, she realized how easy it would be for her to lose her heart to Troy. She'd done some foolish things in her life, but she had a feeling that would be the most foolish.

He might be attracted to her physically but he'd

been clear on more than one occasion that he knew exactly what kind of woman he wanted permanently in his life and she wasn't it.

Still, sleeping with him had been nice. Making love to him had been amazing. She'd awakened once in the night, the vision of the car careening toward her shooting her out of bed with a scream. Troy had calmed her, then had held her close to his chest until she'd fallen asleep again.

She released the pillow and sat up, knowing that today was going to be a difficult one. Not only would she have to contend with baggage from their love-making but she also knew he was going to want to talk about the fact that somebody had tried to kill her the night before.

Just as she'd suspected, her body ached as she stood to leave the room. Her shoulders burned and her back cried out to protest the unaccustomed pull of muscles from the roll down the hill.

She padded naked down the hallway, then went into her bedroom to grab clean clothes for the day. From there she scurried into the bathroom for a shower.

It was just after nine when she entered the kitchen to find Troy seated at the table, an empty cup before him. "Good morning," she said as she walked to the coffeemaker.

She poured herself a cup of the brew, then carried the carafe to where he sat. "Want a refill?"

He nodded. "Thanks."

She filled up his cup, replaced the carafe in the machine, then joined him at the table. "Have you heard from anyone this morning?"

"I checked in with Lucas. Nothing has changed at the house. I also called Kincaid, but he had nothing to report, either."

She took a sip of her coffee. "I have to consider that my father's dead, don't I?" A wealth of emotion filled her chest. It had been four days, and there had been no word, no lead, nothing concerning her father.

Troy held her gaze, a touch of sympathy in the gray depths. "I think you should probably be prepared for anything."

She nodded, grateful that he hadn't tried to put on a smiley face for her. She trusted him to be honest with her, to always be a straight shooter.

He twisted his coffee cup between his hands, hands that had brought her an enormous amount of pleasure the night before, but she had a feeling that whatever thoughts were whirling in his mind wouldn't bring her pleasure at all.

"What are you thinking?" she asked, not sure at all if she wanted to know. She hoped the darkness of his gaze didn't mean they were going to have to have "the talk" about how last night meant nothing, that in the grand scheme of his life, she meant nothing.

He took a sip of the coffee, and when he set the cup down once again, his eyes were even darker. "I think maybe we've been approaching all this from the wrong direction."

She frowned. "What do you mean?"

"I'm talking about the mall development and your father's kidnapping, all of it."

"I don't understand," she replied.

"Your father thought that the attack on you in California and receiving those photos of you were to scare him in his business dealing. He believed that the real target was himself. But this morning I've been sitting here wondering if maybe it has nothing to do with the mall development or any of his business matters."

She frowned, trying to follow his train of thought, but finding it impossible. "Then what would it be about?" she asked.

"You." His gaze held hers intently. "I think maybe it's been about you all along."

"Then why is my dad missing?" she asked.

"Because somebody close to you knew how much it would hurt you." He reached out and covered one of her icy hands with the warmth of his. "Somebody close to you wants to see you cry. They want to see you cry before they see you dead."

She couldn't help the small gasp that escaped her at his words. She wanted to protest, to tell him that he had it all wrong, but the words wouldn't come— because she was terrified that he might be right.

"So what do we do now?" she asked, sorry when he sat back and released her hand.

"We talk about the people in your life, and my gut instinct is that whoever it is isn't in California but rather is here in Kansas City."

She frowned. "But who?"

"Let's start with Kent."

"Kent?" She looked at him in surprise. "Kent would never do anything like this. We're best friends."

"You mentioned that you went to high school with him?"

She nodded. "Actually, we dated all through high school and college."

"And what happened?" He picked up his coffee cup once again.

She shrugged. "Nothing really. I knew Kent wasn't my one great love. I cared about him far more as a friend than as a romantic interest. I moved to California and he stayed here, and we've managed to maintain a wonderful friendship. It was a nice first love that never really matured into anything more."

He took a sip of his coffee, his gaze holding hers over the rim of the cup. "And he didn't have a problem with the relationship changing from romantic to friendship?" he asked as he set the cup back down.

She hesitated before answering. Although Kent had put on a brave face at the time, she'd always had a feeling she'd broken his heart. "I don't know, maybe initially he was hurt by my decision to run off and leave him behind. But that was years ago," she protested.

"Emotions can fester for a long time," he said.

"So you think he's become some sort of psycho stalker?" She couldn't hide her disbelief.

He released a sigh. "I don't know what to think," he confessed. "All I'm telling you is that I think it's time we consider the people closest to you. What about your coworkers at Precious Pets?"

"Sandy and Mike?" She bit back a small laugh as she thought of either of them being crazy killers. "I can't imagine either of them having any reason to want to see me dead."

"Tell me about them."

She leaned back in her chair. "Sandy started working at Precious Pets just after she turned eighteen. She's an avid animal lover, had both office and grooming skills and was good with people. Mike is actually Dr. Mike Kidwell. He's a veterinarian who is as committed to rescuing animals and caring for them as I am. Neither of them would have a reason to want to see me dead. It doesn't make sense, and I hate that you're making me question the loyalty of the people in my life."

"I know. I know none of this is easy," he replied.

"So what's the plan for today?"

"I think we should just sit tight. You need to spend the day making a list of everyone you have dealings with here in Kansas City and anyone from California you think might resent you or be angry with you."

She frowned thoughtfully. "I've always tried to be a good person, to be nice to people and treat them the way I'd want to be treated. I can't imagine anyone doing this to me."

"You have to imagine it because it's happening," he said with a touch of toughness. "There have been two attempts on your life since you've been here in Kansas City, and no state of denial you try to maintain will change that fact. Make a list, Brianna."

She nodded and watched as he got up from the table and carried his cup to the sink. "What are you going to do?"

"I'm going to leave for a little while. I've got a meeting set up with my partners. Unfortunately, we've got other things going on that I need to discuss with them."

She suddenly realized how much he was giving up to be here with her. He hadn't signed up for this, and his life had been placed on hold as much as hers.

"Troy, I'm sorry I got you into this mess. I know you didn't intend to be stuck with me for so long."

He smiled and the gesture lightened the depths of his eyes. "I can't think of anyone else I'd rather be stuck with," he said. His smile fell and he pulled her car keys from his pocket. "I'm going to have to use your vehicle. I had Micah drive mine back to my house the night we went to your father's office."

"No problem, just make sure there isn't a bomb in it before you start it," she said dryly.

"You'll be safe," he said as if to assure her. "Nobody knows you're here."

"I know."

"I should be back by lunchtime."

"Get out of here," she exclaimed. "I'll be fine."

The minute he left the house, Brianna felt his absence deep inside. It scared her just a little, how attached she was becoming to Troy Sinclair.

She had no illusions about the fact that whatever relationship they'd formed in the last week meant nothing, that there would be no happily ever after for the two of them.

He'd been hired by her father to take care of her and he took his commitments seriously. That was probably the only reason why he was still with her, because he was a man of honor and had made a promise to her dad.

Besides, he already knew what kind of woman he wanted to eventually share his life with, and there was no way she could twist herself to fit into the box he'd invented.

She knew he wanted her to use this time to try to figure out who might want her dead. She couldn't imagine Kent harboring some obsessive love-hate attachment that would drive him to want to kill her. Nor could she see Mike Kidwell or Sandy Cartwright being angry with her in any way. The only dealings she had with the two concerned Precious Pets, and she'd never shared a cross word with either of them.

So who?

There was still a part of her that desperately wanted to cling to the fact that this was a result of a business decision her father had made. Otherwise, her father had been kidnapped because of her, and that possibility broke her heart.

Between Troy and her dad, her heart felt as if it had been battered a hundred different ways. One man she could never tell about her growing feelings for him. And she feared she might never again get the chance to tell the other how much she loved him.

"You know you could probably get Kincaid to give Brianna some sort of protection and get yourself out of this assignment?" Micah asked Troy as they sat in the Recovery Inc. office.

Lucas was at the Waverly house, and Micah and Troy had spent the last hour going over pertinent issues concerning their business.

"The police don't have the manpower to watch over her like I can," Troy replied. The idea of anyone else watching over Brianna filled him with a kind of horror. Nobody else would know her like he did. Nobody else would care as much as he did.

He thought of the way she'd fit so perfectly against him as they'd fallen asleep, of that moment when she'd awakened crying and he'd comforted her. Who would hold her if she had another nightmare? Who would soothe her fears if he walked away?

"Brandon hired me and until Brandon releases me, I'm in for the long haul," he said.

Micah gazed at him for a long moment and asked,

"You realize Brandon might not be in a position to release you?" Troy nodded and Micah continued. "How long are you willing to put your life on hold for this particular assignment? And equally important, how long is Brianna willing to stay holed up in the safe house? Eventually she'll want to get back to her life."

"I don't know," Troy answered truthfully. "Right now all I can do is take it one day at a time."

"I'm not sure how long Lucas and I can continue sitting at the Waverly place," Micah said. "We can't let the business suffer because of one job."

"I know," Troy replied. "I told Wendall I didn't want a police presence at the house because of the threat on Waverly's life. I know the police are doing what they can, but I guess it's time for them to be more aggressive." He sighed. "I was hoping this would resolve itself before now. I was also trying to respect Heather's wishes to keep the cops out of it as much as possible, but I'll talk to Brianna about it when I get back to the safe house."

It was only later when he was in the car returning to the safe house that Troy replayed Micah's words in his head.

They couldn't go on like this forever. Although Troy was committed to seeing this through, he certainly couldn't expect his partners to be as committed.

And he and Brianna couldn't continue staying in the safe house while closing out the rest of the world.

Brianna was a woman who wanted the world, who

loved to have her picture taken and hang out in swanky clubs. No matter the risk to her, Troy knew the isolation of the safe house would eventually force her back out into the world. And that thought scared the hell out of him.

Until they knew who was behind the attacks on her, she was vulnerable everywhere she went, with everyone she met. He tightened his hands on the steering wheel. Dammit, they needed a clue. They needed a break that could bring this all to an end.

She'd go back to California and he'd forget that her skin was silky soft, that she had made love to him with a passion that had astounded him. She'd bask in the lights of movie openings and wear little designer gowns that cost more than some people's yearly salaries. And he'd continue to search for the woman of his dreams, the fantasy who had remained elusive so far.

However, none of that could happen unless they could figure out what the hell was going on. So far she'd been reluctant to take a good hard look at her life and see who might have a grudge against her.

If the threat came from somebody who was in her life in California, only she could identify a potential suspect. Whoever that person was, it was obvious they were in Kansas City now, far too close for comfort.

He was completely in the dark and he didn't like it. Maybe she wasn't being honest with him. Maybe there was an old boyfriend who had turned into a psycho stalker.

She'd said there were no old boyfriends except Kent Goodwell, but a woman who looked like Brianna didn't go through life alone. She had to have dated someone else.

He pulled into the driveway of the safe house and got out of the car with a new determination to grill Brianna about her life in California.

He never got the chance. She greeted him at the door, her face flushed and her hand trembling as she grabbed him by the arm.

"What's going on? What's happened?" he asked with alarm.

"I was going through my dad's e-mails," she said as she led him through the living room and into the kitchen. "And I found one from a lawyer. Troy, Dad was divorcing Heather."

She dropped her hand and began to pace the kitchen floor as Troy tried to process what he'd just learned.

"Maybe that's why she refused any help from the cops," Brianna exclaimed, her steps short and quick as she moved from one side of the room to the other. "Maybe she wanted to get rid of Dad before the divorce went through, and maybe she wants to get rid of me while she's still Dad's beneficiary."

She stopped pacing for a moment and faced him, her eyes wild with emotion. "She managed to get rid of me before, now maybe she's trying to make it more permanent."

Chapter Nine

"Brianna, sit down," Troy commanded. "You're making me dizzy." He sat at the table and gestured for her to sit across from him. "What do you mean she got rid of you before?"

She threw herself into the chair, as if finding the confinement abhorrent. She leaned back and drew in a deep breath. "It was Heather's idea that I move to California. When she and Dad first married, she was always reading the tabloids. She'd tell me I was as pretty as all the women who were party dolls in Hollywood. She encouraged me to take off and enjoy my youth. I was so desperate to please her, and to be honest, I was starting to feel like a third wheel. Anyway, I packed my bags and headed off to make her happy."

She raised a trembling hand to shove her hair behind her ear. "This is the first thing that makes sense, Troy. According to the e-mail, Dad had an appointment to go to the lawyer's office next week and finalize his petition for divorce. Heather must have paid somebody to take care of him, and now she wants me dead. If Dad's gone and I'm dead she gets everything, the house, the money and the business."

She jumped up from her chair. "I need to go to the house. I want to see Heather. I need to look her in the face and ask her about the divorce."

Troy didn't attempt to talk her out of it. He knew by the sharp glitter in her eyes, the determined thrust of her chin, that short of bondage there was no way that he was going to keep her from seeing Heather.

She didn't speak again until they were in the car. "It was Heather who didn't want to get the police involved," she exclaimed. "Even when you told her you thought the authorities should be contacted, she's the one who went hysterical and said no."

"But it could just be that she was afraid and wanted to follow the kidnapper's instructions to keep your father alive," he replied, playing devil's advocate.

She shook her head. "It's got to be her, Troy. She has to be the one behind all this."

Troy wasn't sure what to believe, but one thing was certain: Heather's involvement made as much sense as anything else they'd come up with. He knew that divorce cases often turned deadly, especially when there was a fortune involved.

If Brandon's will had Brianna getting half of his fortune, it was possible that Heather wasn't satisfied with the remaining half. Why take a share of the money if you could have it all?

"She's probably been cheating on Dad," Brianna continued. "She probably has some young boyfriend who's helping her in all this. You read about these kinds of things all the time in the newspaper."

Troy could almost smell the angry steam wafting from her. "You need to calm down," he said. "Besides, the police are now watching the house. If Heather's guilty, they'll figure it out."

"I know." She leaned her head back and drew in several deep breaths. "If she's guilty, then Dad is gone. She wouldn't have him kidnapped and kept alive." Her voice caught on a sob.

"Don't jump to conclusions, Brianna. We don't even know that she's responsible. Until we know something for sure, there's still hope." He'd do anything, say anything, to get the anguish out of her voice, off her face.

She flashed him a grateful smile, as if he'd said exactly what she'd needed to hear. She drew another deep breath. "I just want this to be over. I want my dad home, and I want my life back."

"Can't wait to get back to California?"

She surprised him by shaking her head in the negative. "That was never my life. Oh, I'll probably have to go back once more to pack my things, but I'd already decided that it was time for me to get on with my real life, the one I've dreamed about since I was a child."

"And what's that?"

"Living here in Kansas City and running Precious Pets. I was going to tell my father about my decision to come back here, but I never got the chance."

His heart again ached with the pain that laced her voice, but he was also shocked by her words. He'd just assumed she'd go back to California when this was all over. He couldn't imagine her being satisfied here in Kansas City, taking care of a bunch of animals.

She might think that's what she wanted, but he had a feeling it wouldn't take long for Kansas City and her pet project to bore her silly.

"And speaking of Precious Pets, I do intend to be there tomorrow for adoption day," she said.

He cast her a sharp glance, saw that determined thrust of her chin and knew there would be no arguing with her.

"Okay, we'll figure something out."

She sat up straight in the seat as if she hadn't heard him. "I've spent the last six months busting my butt to get donations. I've spent hundreds of dollars on publicity for tomorrow's event. There's no way I'm going to let some creep keep me from being there." She glared at him as if she hadn't heard what he'd just said.

He smiled. "Bree, honey, I said okay. We'll figure it out so you can be there."

She sank back against the seat. "Thank you. Maybe when I confront Heather, she'll confess to everything and then we won't have to worry about me going to the adoption day tomorrow. The guilty will be behind bars, and this will all be truly over."

Troy nodded but he was fairly sure that Heather wasn't going to roll over and confess. He didn't even know if she was the guilty party.

His mind whirled trying to figure out how in the heck he was going to keep Brianna safe at a place where a ton of people might show up to adopt her special pets and one of those people just might be a killer.

As Troy pulled up the street to the Waverly mansion, Brianna sat up straighter in the seat, a renewed burst of anger coursing through her as she thought of her stepmother.

Was it truly possible that Heather could be that evil? That she could have her husband kidnapped and killed, that she could want Brianna dead for money?

There had always been a small part of Brianna that had wondered if Heather had married her father for his money in the first place. She'd wed a man twice her age, and it was only natural to wonder if more than love had motivated her.

"I thought you said the police were watching the house," she said as he pulled into the driveway.

"Trust me, they are." He pointed to a water department van parked down the street. "I'd bet that van isn't filled with pipes and wrenches, but rather with cameras and cops."

He parked the car and grabbed her arm before she

could unfasten her seat belt. "I don't suppose it would do any good to tell you to keep your cool in there."

"Probably not," she exclaimed. "I don't intend to leave here without some answers, and I'm just about in the mood to slap them out of her." She pulled her arm away from his grip, unfastened her seat belt and got out of the car.

She used her key to unlock the door, aware of Troy just behind her, hovering as if he might need to stop her from committing a crime she would regret later.

She felt as if there was an imminent explosion inside her. She wanted to release a primal scream, slap somebody silly, stop being a victim reacting instead of acting.

"Heather!" She walked to the bottom of the staircase, and nodded to Troy's partner Lucas, who had come into the entry. "Heather, come down here right now."

"Sounds like a girl fight on the horizon," Lucas said softly to Troy.

Heather appeared at the top of the stairs. Clad in a long purple duster that set off the red of her hair, her face was wan. "Bree, is there news? Has something happened?"

She hurried down the stairs and reached out for Brianna's hands. Brianna quickly stuck her hands in her pockets, at the same time trying to harden her heart against the woman she'd once wanted to please, a woman she'd thought was a friend.

Heather dropped her hands and moved her gaze from Brianna to Troy. "Mr. Sinclair…is something wrong?"

"Dad was divorcing you," Brianna exclaimed.

She wouldn't have thought it was possible for Heather's face to pale any more, but it did. "Let's go sit down." She motioned them into the living room. "Your father wasn't divorcing me, we were divorcing each other," she said once they were all settled.

A surge of emotion pressed hard in Brianna's chest. When Heather and her father had gotten married she'd been happy, had hoped that her dad had found a lifelong mate, a woman who would spend the rest of her life with him.

"Did you do something to my father?" Brianna kept her voice low. Anger combined with fear and simmered inside her. "Were you afraid he wouldn't be fair with you in the divorce? Have you hired somebody to get rid of me, too?"

The gasp Heather released seemed genuine. "Brianna, how can you think such a thing? Your father and I were going to sit down with you and explain about the divorce. We still love each other, it's just changed into a different kind of love. I would never do anything to hurt your father or you."

"But you refused to get the police involved," Brianna exclaimed.

"The kidnapper said he'd kill Brandon if I brought in the authorities. Maybe I made a mistake, but I was terrified of doing something that might get your father killed."

"Are you seeing somebody else? Do you have a boyfriend?" Brianna asked.

"Absolutely not," Heather said firmly. "Our divorce wasn't about another man or another woman. We've just grown apart. We love each other but we aren't *in* love with each other."

The steam that had worked Brianna up seeped away as she realized nothing would be served by her continuing to badger Heather for answers. If she wasn't guilty then she couldn't help. If she was guilty she wasn't about to announce it to Brianna.

Rushing over here to confront her had been foolish. Brianna stood. "If you didn't have anything to do with this, then I'm sorry. But if you did, then I'll make sure you spend the rest of your life in prison," she exclaimed.

She turned on her heels and headed for the door, half-blinded by a veil of tears. As always Troy was right behind her and as she slid into the passenger side, he got into the driver's seat.

"You okay?" he asked and reached for her hand.

She welcomed the warmth of his hand around hers as she blinked and tears splashed on her cheeks. "I don't know what I expected. Maybe I was looking for a Perry Mason moment, you know where the guilty party breaks down and confesses everything."

"That doesn't happen often in real life." He squeezed her hand, then released it and started the car.

"I want you to talk to your friend Chief Kincaid and tell him that Heather is our most likely suspect," she said.

"I will, but I imagine she's already a likely suspect as far as the police are concerned. Anytime a kidnapping or death occurs, the first person who comes under scrutiny is the spouse."

"As far as I'm concerned her being guilty makes the most sense. No matter how I twist things in my head it's the only thing that makes sense."

"My only concern is keeping you safe. The police will hopefully find out who's responsible for everything, but in the meantime, when we get to the house I've got to figure out how we're going to take care of you being at Precious Pets tomorrow."

She reached out and placed her palm on his thigh. "I realize what an extra burden I'm causing you by insisting I be there tomorrow," she said.

"It's all right. We'll figure something out," he replied.

"I'm glad I'm not going through all this alone, Troy." A new emotion rose up inside her and she realized she was precariously close to falling in love with him.

She yanked her hand away from him, aware that allowing herself to fall for him would be the stupidest thing she'd ever done, and over the past couple of years, she'd done plenty of stupid things.

She should have moved back to Kansas City years ago. She should have been here spending time with her dad and building a life of substance. "You were right about me," she said.

He offered her a quick glance. "Right about what?"

"About me having a lot of opportunities and wasting them doing the party scene in Hollywood. For the past couple of years I kept telling myself that it was time to come home, time to start my real life, but there was a part of me that enjoyed the parties and clubs, the glitz and glamour."

He smiled, the gesture softening his features. "So what you're confessing to is that you're human?"

"I've been stupid," she replied. "I could have been here spending time with my dad and taking care of my business. I'm twenty-nine years old, and I don't even have a boyfriend. I didn't realize until just now how much my life has been on hold."

"It's not too late for you," he replied with a touch of humor. "You aren't exactly over-the-hill. There's still plenty of time for you to find a boyfriend, take care of your business and build a life for yourself."

"I know. It's just that without my father, it will never be the same." Once again tears burned at her eyes and she swallowed hard against them, refusing to give in to the fear, the uncharacteristic vulnerability that tried to take hold of her. "I haven't even been out to Precious Pets to see Big Sam."

"Big Sam?"

"He's a golden retriever who thinks he's in charge of Precious Pets and owns a large chunk of my heart."

She warmed at thoughts of the dog. "Two years ago I rescued him from a man who was going to put him in the pound because he could no longer take care of him. Big Sam and I bonded instantly. I try to get back here four or five times a year and spend time with him. Eventually, when I find a place with a big fenced yard, he's going to live with me."

"I've heard that goldens make terrific pets."

She nodded. "Almost every dog has the potential to be a terrific pet. The nice thing about animals is that they don't judge. They don't care where you've been or what you've done. As long as you feed and water them and love them, they love you back. It's the most uncomplicated relationship anyone can have."

"Uncomplicated, that's what I want in my relationships," he replied.

His words served to remind her that she would never be, could never be, the woman he wanted for a long-term relationship.

The wave of despair that had threatened to engulf her moments before now descended upon her like a black cloud, stealing any hint of sunshine.

Chapter Ten

It was just after nine when Troy pulled into the lane that led to the Precious Pets establishment. Although the public party planned for today wasn't set to begin until one that afternoon, he figured the easiest way to assure Brianna's safety was to get there early and look things over.

He'd made sure they hadn't been followed from the safe house and he saw no potential threat when he parked his car.

"Mike's already here," Brianna said and pointed to the pickup truck parked on the side of the building. "He's probably doing last-minute health checks on all the animals."

Together they got out of Brianna's SUV and as they began to walk toward the long one-story building Brianna released a musical whistle.

The dog appeared in the distance next to Mike's truck. He was a beautiful golden retriever and when he saw Brianna he came bounding toward them.

"Big Sam," she called with a laugh of sheer pleasure. As the dog reached her, he jumped and she landed on her back in the grass, girlish giggles escaping her as Big Sam greeted her with frantic tail wags and lavish kisses.

This was the picture of her that would remain with Troy for a very long time to come. A beautiful woman whose laughter rode the breeze as she hugged the big dog in unabandoned delight.

She got to her feet, a hand on top of the dog's head. "Big Sam, sit," she instructed. The dog complied. "Say hello to Troy." Big Sam barked and held out a paw for a shake.

Troy laughed and shook the dog's paw. "Hello, Big Sam." He grinned at Brianna. "He's a beauty."

She nodded. "And smart as a whip."

"Let's get you inside," he said, not wanting to linger in the openness of the yard. No sense in tempting fate. Although he sensed no threat, he hadn't forgotten that on the day that somebody had shot at them at the job site, he hadn't sensed a threat, either.

Precious Pets was divided into two areas. The first was a large reception room with a counter behind which a receptionist worked. The second and largest area was in the back room. There were three wide aisles of cages and kennels.

"How many animals do you have?" he asked Mike Kidwell, who showed him around the back.

"Right now we have sixty. We like to keep it

around fifty or under." The nice-looking veterinarian smiled, his brown eyes friendly. "I'm hoping we can find a good home for at least ten or fifteen dogs and cats today."

"Brianna seems passionate about all this."

"She is. She's great. I think it's awesome that she's poured so much of her money into this place. She's also been successful in getting us plenty of donations to keep us up and running."

"She's in a bit of trouble," Troy said. "You know somebody took a shot at her the other day, then somebody tried to run her over with a car."

Mike's eyes widened. "Why? What's going on?"

"We don't know, but I thought I'd give you a heads-up that I've got half a dozen undercover cops showing up today for extra security." Thank God Wendall Kincaid had agreed to send men for the afternoon. "There won't be a minute today that Brianna isn't covered by either a cop or me."

"Is there anything I can do to help?" Mike asked.

Troy smiled. "Yeah, get twenty of these mutts adopted out."

Mike grinned. "Before I can do that, I've got to get them all outside and into pens where people can view them."

"I'll just get out of your way so you can get back to it." Troy left Mike and returned to the front area where Brianna was seated at the receptionist desk and talking on the phone.

"I want you set up no later than twelve-thirty," she said to whoever was on the other end of the line. "And I'd rather have too many hot dogs than not enough. And plenty of relish. I love relish on my hot dogs. Okay, we'll see you then." She hung up and smiled at Troy. "That was Bart of Bart's Hot Dogs and Fun. We're going to have hot dogs and cotton candy and popcorn during the afternoon."

"You've gone to a lot of trouble for this," he said as he sat in a chair near the desk.

"I've advertised it as a day of family fun. Come see the animals, enjoy the food and music."

"Music?"

"I didn't mention the deejay, did I? He's supposed to be here around noon to set up."

"I had no idea this was going to be such a big extravaganza," Troy said.

She leaned back in the chair and tucked a strand of her hair behind her ear. "I've been working on this for months. It's not just about adopting animals, it's also to let people know we're here, that we're a viable option instead of the pound. We have no death sentence here. No animals are put down unless it's absolutely necessary because of health issues. We have a drop-off pen outside where people can leave animals with no questions asked." She frowned. "I just wish…" She let her voice trail off.

He knew what she wished. "He would be so proud of you," he said.

She flashed him a bittersweet smile. "I know. Even though we've been here for almost three years, we've never had anything like this to let people know about us. After today I'm hoping everyone in Kansas City knows about Precious Pets."

The morning flew by as Troy followed Brianna around while she checked pens inside and out, petted and loved every dog in the place and double-checked last-minute details.

Sandy arrived at eleven, her blond hair worn in the same style as Brianna and clad in a blouse that looked remarkably similar to one that he'd seen Brianna wearing in the tabloid photos. It was obvious she had a severe case of hero worship.

By twelve-thirty the place looked as if a party was about to occur. The deejay had set up his equipment and was testing it, the air was redolent with the scents of cooking hot dogs, sweet cotton candy and popcorn. The dogs and cats were all in pens outside, producing a cacophony of sound that rivaled the deejay's rock and roll.

At twelve-thirty Troy went to the back room where a few dogs still remained in their pens, dogs that were sick or not deemed fully ready for adoption. He walked over to a window that provided a view of the back of the property, an area that was heavily wooded.

He heard the soft sound of footsteps, smelled the familiar scent of perfume and knew that Brianna had joined him. "How far back does your property go?"

"Acres and acres," she replied as she came to stand beside him. "I haven't even been back to the property line. It's thick woods and brush. Eventually I'd like to clear some of it off and expand. Maybe set up a training area and hire somebody to train working dogs for the blind and such."

He looked at her. Her hair was mussed and the lipstick she'd worn out of the house that morning had long since disappeared. The faint scent of wet dog mingled with her perfume, and he thought she'd never looked so lovely.

"You've got big dreams," he observed.

She smiled. "Are there any other kind? What about you, Troy? What kind of dreams do you have?"

"None. I like things just as they are in my life." He felt the need to distance himself from her, from the swell of desire for her that suddenly filled him. "It's almost one. We'd better get up front."

How long would a Hollywood socialite be happy here in Kansas City running an animal shelter? He gave it two, three months tops before she went running back to her designer clothes and fancy friends.

The undercover cops arrived and were briefed by Troy, and at one o'clock, all that was missing were people. "What if nobody shows up?" Brianna asked worriedly as she gazed out the front window.

"Don't worry, people will show up," Sandy said. "If nothing else some people will come just to see you."

Brianna smiled at the young woman. "I don't want people coming for me. I want them here for the animals." She turned back to the window. "Here comes a car," she exclaimed. "It's Kent!" Before Troy could stop her, she raced out of the door.

He started after her, then relaxed as he saw two of the undercover cops following her. Troy watched from the window as she threw herself into the arms of the handsome, dark-haired young man that stepped out of the car.

Kent would be Kent Goodwell, the man she'd dated through high school, the one she'd been dating when she'd left for California. He was a good-looking guy and carried himself with an air of confidence. Troy was stunned by the alien emotion that filled him, one he identified as jealousy.

How could he be jealous when he was so certain Brianna wasn't the right woman for him? He clenched his jaw and reminded himself that she was just a job, not his fantasy woman. He definitely had to get a grip on himself, he thought.

He watched as the two of them came inside, Brianna with a beatific smile on her face. "Troy, this is my good friend Kent. And Kent, this is Troy Sinclair, a friend and at the moment my bodyguard."

Kent looked at him with surprise and held out his hand. "Bodyguard?" he asked as he shook Troy's hand.

"It's a long story," Brianna replied.

Kent smiled at Brianna. "Then we definitely have to make some time to catch up on things."

"There's more cars coming in," Sandy said from the front window.

"We'll talk about it later," Brianna said to Kent.

Kent was still in love with her, Troy thought as he noticed the handsome man watching Brianna. It was obvious in the man's eyes, in the way he touched her whenever possible.

As the day of festivity began, Troy couldn't help but notice how Kent was never far from Brianna's side, how he hung on her every word and watched her when she wasn't aware of him.

Troy had a feeling there were plenty of unresolved emotions where Kent was concerned. What he didn't know was whether those emotions had somehow spiraled out of control, transformed a love relationship into an obsessive hate.

It certainly wouldn't be anything new, the mental state of "If he couldn't have her, nobody else could." Time and time again the papers and crime annals were filled with such stories.

What he had to figure out was if Kent Goodwell was really a viable suspect or if his brain was clouded by the unexpected surge of jealousy.

"TWENTY-THREE DOGS AND CATS," Brianna exclaimed as she threw her arms around Troy's neck. "That's how many found homes today."

The hot-dog man had gone home, the deejay was packing up and the guests who had filled the grounds for the last three hours had all departed.

She stepped back from him when he didn't return the embrace. "Are you okay?"

"Just tired," he replied. "I'm glad the day was such a huge success for you."

"Not for me, for the animals. We need to celebrate," she replied. "If I was back in California, I'd say let's go get some champagne and dance the night away, but since we can't do that how about we stop on the way home and pick up a bottle of wine and a frozen pizza?"

Before he could reply, Mike walked into the office, a tired but triumphant smile on his face. "Why don't you two go ahead and get out of here? Sandy and I can finish things up."

"Are you sure?" Brianna asked.

"Go," Mike commanded. "Go home and relax. There's not much left to do. Sandy and I will be out of here within a half an hour."

"Okay," she replied. She felt as if she were covered in animal hair and dirt. What she wanted more than anything at the moment was a nice, hot bath.

Together she and Troy left the building and headed toward the car. When they were both buckled in, Troy turned and looked at her. "He's still in love with you."

She frowned. "Who?"

"Kent. He's still in love with you."

"We're friends. He loves me, but he's not *in* love with me," she replied, surprised by the very topic of conversation.

"I'm telling you that man is in love with you." Troy's jaw knotted and she stared at him in surprise.

"Okay, whatever. But I'm not in love with him and he knows that." What was with him? He was acting almost like a jealous lover.

She scoffed inwardly at this ridiculous thought. She wasn't even sure Troy Sinclair really liked her; why would he be jealous of an old boyfriend?

Troy started the car and they headed down the lane toward the highway. "What are you thinking?" she asked, wishing she could read his thoughts. In all the time they'd spent together, she had never felt such distance from him like she did now.

"I'm just wondering how obsessed Kent really is with you, if he's obsessed enough to want you dead rather than with anyone else."

"That's crazy," she exclaimed. She stared out the side window, his words echoing in her head. Was the idea any crazier than anything they'd come up with so far? "If it is Kent, then why would he kidnap my father?"

"I don't know. Maybe to hurt you? Maybe to keep you in town longer. He knows as long as your father is missing you won't fly back to California. Maybe he intended to be your hero, your support while you were worried about your dad."

"You have an evil mind," she exclaimed.

His lips pressed together in a grim smile. "Sometimes you have to think evil to find evil." At that moment, his cell phone rang. He answered and listened for a long minute. "Yeah, all right. Got it."

He hung up and slipped the phone back in the pocket of his sports shirt, then cast a quick glance in her direction. "That was Kincaid. They got an anonymous call that if they want to find Brandon, they should look at Sandy Cartwright's place."

"Sandy?" Brianna thought of the young woman who worked for her. She sat up straighter in her seat. "We have to go there. I know where she lives." An anonymous call? Who could have made such a call?

Although it made no sense that Sandy would be involved in any of this, a desperate urgency filled Brianna. Was it possible they were finally going to get some answers?

"It's probably best if we let the police handle it," Troy said.

"Turn left at the highway," she said. "Sandy's place is only fifteen minutes from here."

Troy released a sigh. "Why do I sometimes think when I'm talking to you that nobody is listening?"

"I listen," she protested. "But you should know me well enough by now to realize that when you told me that information, I was going to make you take me directly to Sandy's place."

"You're right, I knew that," he agreed. Once again his lips compressed tightly together.

Maybe he was getting tired of this, tired of her. At the thought a sudden dart of pain shot through her and she realized just how deeply Troy Sinclair had crawled into her heart.

She forced her gaze out the passenger window. She couldn't think about that now. She had to focus on the fact that this was the first real lead they'd had concerning her father.

"Maybe they can trace the call, find out who made it," she said.

"Time will tell," he replied.

Even though she had no idea what relationship Sandy might have with her father, even though Sandy was the last person she would suspect in any crime in the city, her mind whirled with possibilities.

Heather and her father were divorcing. Was it possible that her father and Sandy had begun a relationship? No, Brianna couldn't imagine her father dating somebody younger than her. He just wasn't that kind of man.

"Turn left at the next corner," she said. The closer they got to the old farmhouse where Sandy lived, the more an edge of wild hope built up inside Brianna. Please let him be there, she prayed. And let him be alive.

She closed her eyes and imagined her father's thick, strong arms around her, his familiar scent of expensive cologne, breath mints and cigars surrounding her.

Someplace deep inside her she knew how unlikely it was that he'd be found alive, but her heart refused to relinquish the tiny flicker of hope that still burned.

Kent. Sandy. Heather. James Stafford. The names of suspects whirled in her head. Which one would want to kidnap her father, and which one might want her dead?

She examined one, then discarded the thought in favor of another, her mind jumbled and confused as it worked to find answers. "Turn right at the next intersection," she said, breaking the taut silence that had descended in the car. "Sandy's farmhouse is about five miles ahead on the right."

"She lives in a farmhouse? She seems awfully young. Does she live there with her parents?" Troy asked.

"No, she lives alone. Her grandparents left her the place a couple of years ago, and she's lived there since their deaths."

"It's pretty isolated out here," he observed as they passed fields of corn and then a stand of trees.

"It's a perfect place to keep a kidnapped person without anyone knowing it," she replied.

"Don't get your hopes up, Brianna. This is probably a wild-goose chase, maybe the kidnapper having a little fun. Sandy doesn't strike me as the criminal type."

Brianna thought of the young woman who had lightened her hair to the same shade as hers. Sandy had always struck her as sweet if a bit immature. "I know, I'm trying not to get my hopes up, but this is the first communication we've had from the kidnapper since his initial call to Heather."

"We're not even sure the anonymous call really came from the kidnapper," he reminded her. "The police get all kinds of crazy calls in instances like this."

"But they're taking it seriously enough to check it out," she replied.

When they pulled onto the lane that led to the small farmhouse, three police cars were already parked in front. It didn't appear that any search had begun yet. The officers were clustered on the porch, along with a tall, dark-haired man in a suit.

"The suit is Chief Wendall Kincaid," Troy said as he put the SUV in park and shut off the engine.

Brianna wanted to jump out of the car and beat down the door to search the rooms, but a sudden, throat-choking fear held her in place.

She looked at Troy and he must have seen the emotion in her eyes, in the tension of her facial features, because he reached out and took her hand.

She swallowed hard. "I'm suddenly terrified," she confessed. "I'm afraid we'll find him and he'll be dead, and I'm afraid we won't find him and the uncertainty will just go on and on." She stared at the house, where Wendall Kincaid and a uniformed officer detached from the group and were heading toward their vehicle.

Troy released her hand. "Come on, let's find out

what's going on." Together they got out of the car and met Wendall.

"We're waiting for one of two things," Wendall explained. "We need either a search warrant or Sandra Cartwright's permission to search the place."

"She's at Precious Pets, but she should be here within a half an hour," Brianna said. Her stomach twisted in knots. She didn't want to wait. "Why can't you just go on in? Break down the door and see if my dad is there?"

Wendall's dark eyes held a touch of sympathy. "Because that's illegal."

"So is kidnapping," Brianna exclaimed.

"Yes, but our doing that would jeopardize a trial down the line. I understand that you're anxious, but we have to do things the right way."

Brianna released a sigh of impatience and at the same time welcomed Troy's arm around her shoulder. "Patience, Bree," he said softly.

She sagged against him, wondering how long she could maintain this level of emotional intensity without breaking. At that moment Sandy pulled into the driveway. She got out of the car, a confused and slightly frightened look on her face.

"What's going on? Why are the police here?" Her voice was thin and higher pitched than usual.

"We've received some information and would like to conduct a search of the premises," Wendall said to her.

"A search? For what?" Her gaze darted frantically from Wendall to Brianna, then back to Wendall.

"I'm not at liberty to discuss the details," Wendall said. He offered her a charming smile. "It's probably nothing, but we really need to do this. Would you give us permission to search?"

She hesitated and in that hesitation Brianna felt as if she might throw up. Although she couldn't imagine Sandy being responsible for her father's kidnapping, was it possible she was involved with the kidnapper?

"All right, of course," she finally said. She handed Wendall her key ring. "The gold one unlocks the front door."

Wendall handed the key to the uniformed officer, who hurried toward the front door. "It would be easier if you all just wait out here," he said. He turned his gaze to Sandy. "We'll be as careful as possible with your personal space."

"If you could just tell me what you're looking for, maybe all this isn't necessary," she said. "I don't do drugs. Is that what this is about?"

Troy held tight to Brianna, as if to keep her silent and let Wendall handle things. Before Wendall could reply, an officer stepped out on the porch. "Chief, you might want to come in here."

An urgency in the officer's voice shot through Brianna. She broke free from Troy's hold and ran toward the house.

"Brianna, wait! I need to explain," Sandy cried after her.

Explain? Explain what? Horrible thoughts flashed through Brianna's mind as she ran toward the front door of the house, desperately afraid of what lay within.

Chapter Eleven

Troy raced after her, his heart beating so hard, so loudly he scarcely heard Wendall calling after them or Sandy's hysterical cries.

Brianna disappeared into the house as he took the porch steps in two long strides. He entered a living room that was neat and tidy. An officer stood at the doorway that led into the kitchen but the activity came from a room down the hallway.

With Wendall at his heels, Troy shoved through the throng of policemen and entered a small bedroom where Brianna stood in the center, her hands clasped over her mouth in obvious shock.

It took only one glance around the room for him to see what had shocked her. All four walls had been papered with pictures of her. They'd obviously been cut out of tabloids and gossip magazines and taped to the walls to create the montage of obsession.

"What the hell?" Wendall stepped into the room and looked around.

Sandy followed him, hysterical sobs ripping through her as she started toward Brianna. Troy stepped between the two, unsure what was going on, but knowing the last place he wanted Sandy was near Brianna.

"I'm so embarrassed," Sandy cried. "Please, Bree, I haven't done anything wrong. I don't know why you're here, but I would never do anything to hurt you."

"Check the rest of the house and the outbuildings," Wendall said to the men who had gathered in the doorway.

"Please, believe me," Sandy said to Brianna. "I just admire you so much. I've been studying your pictures, trying to find clothes like yours. I think you're wonderful, Bree. I just wanted to be like you." Deep sobs shook her shoulders as she hid her face in her hands.

"Admire me?" Brianna's face radiated a mix of emotions, disbelief coupled with revulsion. "You admire me for this?" She swept her hands out to encompass the walls.

Before anyone could stop her, she began to tear at the pictures, pulling them off the wall and ripping them in half. Stunned, nobody moved to stop her as she worked more and more frantically, destroying the pictures as tears coursed down her cheeks.

"This is just Saturday night in Hollywood. Don't admire me for this," she cried. "This isn't who I am or what I do."

It was finally Troy who grabbed her in his arms

and held her. She fought him, struggling to get out of his embrace, but he held tight, refusing to let her go.

She looked up at him, frustration shining from her tear-filled eyes. "It's just Saturday night, not the rest of the days of the week," she said as she stopped struggling.

"I know," he replied. Aware that the fight had left her, he dropped his arms from around her.

Brianna pushed past Troy and walked to Sandy. "It's all right. I understand."

"I didn't mean any harm. I promise I wouldn't ever do anything to hurt you," Sandy exclaimed.

"Sandy, if you're going to admire me, do it because I'm nice to people or because I'm passionate about animals. But don't admire me because I get dressed up and somebody takes pictures of me," Brianna said.

She looked at Troy. "Let's go home. I don't think they'll find anything here." She didn't wait for his response but turned and left the room, her shoulders slumped in utter defeat.

Troy followed behind her, a simmering anger building up inside him. He had no idea what had provoked it, wasn't sure where it was directed, but it remained thick in his chest as he and Brianna got back into her vehicle.

They didn't speak for the first five minutes of the drive back to the safe house. Troy tightly gripped the steering wheel as a building pressure grew inside him.

He tried to seek the source, wondered if it was a residual sentiment from the unexpected surge of jealousy he'd experienced earlier concerning Kent.

Or maybe it was seeing all those photographs of Brianna plastered all over Sandy's walls. In all probability Sandy's obsession with the famous Bree Waverly was probably benign, but he couldn't help but wonder how many other creeps might have developed similar, less innocent kinds of obsessions with her.

"That was more than a little creepy," Troy said.

"She wouldn't hurt anybody. I always knew she kind of had a girl crush on me. Poor Sandy," she said. "I hope she doesn't quit over all this. She's great with the animals and the bookkeeping, and she's such a sweet girl."

"That's all you're worried about? That she might quit?" he asked. He was feeling dangerously on edge, teetering on a precipice of sheer emotion.

"Well, of course that's not all I'm worried about," she exclaimed.

"What you should be worried about is how many other creeps have your pictures up on their walls. You put yourself out there, dressed in skimpy outfits and dripping sex appeal, then throw up your hands in surprise when you become the victim of a stalker or a nut."

"It's not like I'm the only woman in Hollywood making the tabloids," she said.

"No, but you're the only one I've made love with.

You're the only one I care about." He tightened his lips together and clutched the steering wheel.

Dammit, he hadn't meant to say that. He felt her staring at him as he pulled up and parked in front of the safe house. "It's my job to keep you safe," he said as if she'd asked for an explanation. "But your lifestyle and past actions are making this more difficult."

"Don't you dare try to make this my fault, Troy," she said as she got out of the car. She slammed the car door with more force than necessary.

Troy followed her up to the porch, knowing he'd made her angry and welcoming this new tension between them. He needed some distance, from her and from the situation.

Things were spiraling out of control and he hated the feeling of helplessness that filled him. She was making him crazy; he wanted her and he hated it because he was afraid for her and for her father.

As he unlocked the door, she swept in before him and went right to her bedroom where she slammed the door shut with enough force to shake the windows in their frames.

He threw himself on the sofa and hoped she'd stay in her bedroom for the next ten years. He didn't know why she was so deep under his skin at the moment, but she was and he just needed her to stay away from him for a little while.

She exited the bedroom only to stomp into the

bathroom, and a moment later he heard the sound of the water running in the shower.

He leaned his head back and closed his eyes. Instantly his mind created a vision of her standing naked beneath a steamy spray with her hair slicked back to display her high cheekbones, that perfect nose and those lush lips.

It was at that moment he recognized the source of his anger. It was born of desire. He wanted her again, and he hated himself for it. He'd lost all his objectivity where she was concerned. It was messing with his mind on a personal level, and it was screwing him up on a professional level.

He no longer knew if the threat to her came from the way she'd lived her life in California or the way her father had conducted business. He didn't know if it was an old boyfriend or a community activist. She'd scrambled his mind to a point that he didn't know which end was up anymore.

He tensed as the sound of the shower water went off. Maybe she'd go back in the bedroom, he thought. Of course, she didn't do what he wanted, but instead marched back into the living room and faced him.

Clad only in her pale pink robe and a self-righteous anger, she looked glorious. "You're a fine one to talk about personal choices and lifestyles, Troy Sinclair," she exclaimed.

He narrowed his eyes and stood. "What are you talking about?"

"I'm talking about the fact that you're thirty-five years old and not married because you have some fantasy woman in your mind. Maybe the real reason you're still alone is because you're afraid of having a real relationship with a real woman."

"You don't know what you're talking about," he scoffed. "Besides, you're almost thirty and I don't see a significant other in your life."

She flushed but raised her chin even higher. "At least I don't have some crazy fantasy in my head that will be impossible to find. All I want is a man who will love the fact that I like animals and designer high heels, who will accept that I sometimes made mistakes in my past. I want a man who will love me despite the fact that I'm complex and can be difficult."

She stopped and drew in a deep breath, her forehead wrinkling with perplexity. "Why are we fighting?"

Troy sat back on the sofa, some of the tension ebbing out of him. "I'm not sure. Maybe as a stress reliever."

"There's got to be a better way to release stress," she replied and sat next to him.

Troy could definitely think of a better way, but making love with her again would only complicate things further.

"This can't go on," she said softly. She leaned her head against the back of the sofa cushion. "You need to get back to your real life, and I need to get out of your hair. My suggestion is first thing tomorrow morning you take me home. I'll be safe there." She reached over and covered Troy's hand with hers. "You've done your job, Troy. It wasn't supposed to be a lifetime assignment. It was just supposed to be a couple of days."

He'd just been thinking he needed to distance himself from her and she was giving him the perfect opening. He could walk away from her and this assignment with no harm, no foul. So why did the very idea make his heart feel heavy?

BRIANNA STARED AT TROY'S elegant features, the blond buzz-cut hair that looked stiff yet was soft beneath her touch, the slate gray eyes that could be warm and welcoming or icy with contempt.

She was in love with him, and she was caught between the need to run as far away from him as possible and the desire to throw herself in his arms and confess how she felt. But she knew doing the latter would be foolish.

Why burden him with her feelings when she knew, had always known, that she wasn't the woman he wanted to spend his life with, wasn't even close to the fantasy woman he held in his mind?

"Why would you want to go back home?" he asked. "Wouldn't it bother you to be there with Heather? She hasn't been ruled out as a suspect."

"The more I think about it, the less I think Heather had anything to do with Dad's disappearance. For one thing, I'm not sure she's smart enough to pull off something like this." Besides, being with Heather would certainly be easier than being here with Troy, she thought.

"Look, today has been an emotional roller coaster," he said. "The high of the adoption celebration, the drama of thinking you might find your dad—maybe we should wait until morning before we make any decisions about where we go from here."

She knew he was probably right, that her emotions were crazy right now, because all she really wanted was for him to sweep her up in his arms and carry her into his bedroom and make love to her until dawn.

"I'm sure your family misses you," she replied.

He smiled, a tired gesture that didn't quite reach his eyes. "My family is used to me disappearing for days at a time."

She curled her legs up beneath her. "I used to call my dad every Sunday from California."

"It must have been hard on you, when your father married Heather."

Brianna frowned thoughtfully. "Yes and no. It had been just Dad and me for a long time, but as I got older, I knew Dad was lonely. I was actually happy when he married Heather. I liked the idea of him having somebody to share his life with, somebody who would be with him as he grew old."

The tension that had been in the air between them since they'd returned to the house was gone, and instead she felt just a quiet weariness, a knowledge that it was time for the two of them to part ways, before her heart got any more tangled on a path that could only lead to heartache. And she was afraid that there was already a wealth of heartache for her to face.

The hope she'd been able to maintain about her father still being alive could no longer find purchase inside her. But she didn't want to think about that now, couldn't stand facing what might be ahead.

"Talk to me about your life, Troy. Tell me what movies you like, what you enjoy doing on Saturday nights." She heard the quiet desperation in her voice.

He must have heard it too, and understood her need to be taken away from the drama, from the horror of what had become her life.

He spent the next hour telling her stories about his childhood and his three sisters. He made her laugh and in those moments she fell in love with him just a little bit more.

"What about you?" he asked. "What was your life like in California? When you were ripping those pictures off Sandy's walls, you said that they just depicted one night of the week, not the rest of the days and nights."

She smiled. "You'd be surprised by how normal it was. I spent a lot of my days contacting people about Precious Pets, getting promises for donations and such. On Tuesday and Thursday nights, I went to a Pilates class. I watched a lot of television, did a lot of reading. I love to read. I met friends for coffee, got groceries, ate out. It was a normal life for the most part. That's what people who read the tabloids and gossip magazines don't realize, that those pictures are just one night in the lives of those people."

She frowned thoughtfully. "Sure, there are some Hollywood types who are more than a little crazy themselves, who definitely don't live normal lives, but I wasn't one of them."

"I've noticed that you don't get many calls on your cell phone."

"I keep that particular number private. The only people who have it are a few friends and Dad and Heather."

"So you haven't heard from your friends back in Hollywood?"

"I didn't expect to," she admitted. "Most of the people I hung out with were more acquaintances than friends. It would definitely be a case of out of sight, out of mind with them." As it would be with Troy, she thought. In all probability when he took her back to her house tomorrow, she wouldn't cross his mind again. His job would be done and that was that.

And it was in those moments that she recognized how difficult it would be to tell him goodbye the next morning. By nine o'clock she got up from the sofa. "I'm exhausted," she said. "It's been a long day."

He stood and stretched with his arms overhead. "Yeah, it has been a long day." She waited as he turned out the lights and checked the doors to make sure they were locked, then together they walked down the hallway.

"Good night, Brianna," he said as they reached the doorway to the room where she'd been sleeping.

Knowing that the next day she'd tell him goodbye, knowing that she was already walking away with more than a little bit of a bruised heart, what she wanted from him at that moment wasn't a simple good-night, but rather a final memory to carry with her when she walked away from him the next day.

"Troy." His name fell from her lips as a plea, and as she stepped closer to him he opened his arms as if he'd expected her, welcomed her.

His mouth claimed hers with a fervent appetite and she responded with a hunger of her own. She molded against him and felt his instant response, and she knew that even though she wasn't the woman he wanted forever, she was the woman he wanted at this very moment.

It was enough for her, because it had to be enough. She wrapped her arms more tightly around his neck, wanting to lose herself in him.

When the kiss finally ended, she took his hand and pulled him into the bedroom. "Troy, make love to me," she whispered. "This night is all we have left and I want you. I need you."

The wanting was naked on his handsome features. His eyes burned with it, his body tensed with it, and yet she felt his hesitation. "You're going to take me home in the morning. Tomorrow you get your life back but tonight you're mine."

She wouldn't have thought it possible for his eyes to flame hotter, but they did and without saying a word he began to unbutton his shirt.

As he undressed, she did the same and together they slid beneath the sheets and reached for one another again.

He knew where to kiss her, how to touch her to evoke the most pleasure, and she wanted to weep as her love for him buoyed up inside her, filling her to such a degree that there was no room for anything else.

It was as if they had been lovers for years and yet had maintained the excitement, the adventure of new lovers. She kissed him with desperation, with a shivering need to indelibly burn this not only into her own mind but also into his.

She wrapped her legs around his, loving the feel of his warm nakedness against her. She memorized his scent, knowing that if she ever smelled his particular brand of cologne again she would immediately be assailed by thoughts of this night in his arms.

As his mouth took hers again, she ran her fingers over his silklike short hair and down the broad width of his back. She felt so safe in his arms, as if it were where she belonged forever. But forever ended when the sun rose again and she intended to savor each and every moment of this final time with him.

His hands moved to her breasts, where he used his

thumbs to caress her nipples until she thought she'd scream. Each and every touch evoked sweet sensations that kept her breathless and achingly needy.

As his hand left her breast and traveled the length of her abdomen, a new, more urgent tension filled her. She arched up to meet his touch and whispered his name in the darkness of the room.

He was a thoughtful lover, both passionate and gentle, demanding and giving. She knew instinctively that there would never come a time that his touch didn't excite her, warm her to the core of her being.

At that moment her cell phone rang. Troy froze. "Just ignore it," she exclaimed, not wanting to lose the moment.

"You need to answer. It might be something important." His voice was low, thick with lingering desire.

He rolled away from her and she wanted to scream in frustration. He grabbed her cell from the nightstand and handed it to her.

As she flipped it open she was aware of Troy getting out of bed and reaching for his clothing. Whatever had been about to happen between them was over.

The caller ID read anonymous but she flipped it open and answered. "Hello?"

"Brianna, this is Mike." There was an urgency in his voice that shot her to an upright position. "I'm sorry to bother you but in the craziness of the afternoon apparently I forgot to get Big Sam into his kennel. I just stopped by Precious Pets to check things out before calling it a night and he's here, but it looks like he's been hit by a car. It's bad, Brianna. I think you should get right over here."

"We'll be right there," she exclaimed and quickly hung up.

"What happened?" Troy asked, already dressed in his slacks and reaching for his shirt.

She flew out of bed, her heart hammering with anxiety. "It's Big Sam. Mike thinks he's been hit by a car." She grabbed a pair of jogging pants from the drawer and yanked them on, then pulled on a T-shirt.

She made it to the door before the tears welled up and exploded out of her. Not Big Sam. Please, don't take him away from her.

Suddenly she was sobbing, not just out of fear for Big Sam, but for her missing father, for the loss of the family she thought she'd known and finally because she loved a man who she knew wouldn't, couldn't love her back.

Chapter Twelve

Troy pulled her against his chest and held her. She leaned into him with a trust and a vulnerability that humbled him.

He should have seen this coming, her tears, her utter defeat. Up until now she'd shown amazing strength and control. She'd met each and every dead end, each and every threat with a stiff upper lip and a sense of humor, but now both seemed to have abandoned her.

Since the moment they'd left Sandy's farmhouse, he should have realized how fragile she was. He should have anticipated that anything might have the capacity to shove her into a breakdown.

Her angry display at Sandy's, replaced by her frantic need to make love, had all pointed to the rain of tears that now possessed her. It was all too much for her and he wished there was a way he could take on some of her grief, shoulder it for her, but he knew he couldn't.

She sobbed out a lifetime of grief in a span of two

or three minutes. He held her close, murmured non-sensical comfort into her ear and patted her back.

Although he was worried about the dog, he was also grateful that the phone call had halted their love-making before it had actually happened.

He'd been about to make love to her without any protection, without any thought of consequences. They'd been about to make a mistake that they might have paid for for the rest of their lives.

"If anything happens to Big Sam, I don't know what I'll do," she cried into the front of his shirt as her fingers bit into his shoulders. "I can't stand the thought of losing him, too."

He knew that her tears were for more than the beloved dog, but there was nothing he could say to convince her that her world would ever be right again.

"Brianna." He gently took her by the shoulders and held her back from him. "You told me Mike is a terrific vet, and I'm sure he'll do everything in his power to save Big Sam, but we need to go in case he needs help."

She nodded and as she raised her face to look at him again he tenderly swiped at her tears. As he stared into her misty blue eyes, he realized she would haunt him for a long time to come.

Minutes later they were in his car and headed down the two-lane highway that led to Precious Pets.

A full moon cast down from a cloudless sky as Troy drove as fast as possible without putting them at risk. As always he kept an eye on the rearview mirror, making sure they weren't followed, but at this time of night and on these country roads, there were no other cars except theirs.

Neither of them spoke for several minutes, then it was Troy who broke the silence. "Tomorrow before I take you home I'll contact Kincaid. He'll see to it that you have twenty-four-hour police protection until they can figure out what's going on."

He hadn't been sure until now if he was going to agree with her decision to return home in the morning, but after almost falling into bed with her again, he knew it was best for both of them.

Still, even as he said the words, he felt a strange kind of despair. And in that despair he realized how much he'd wanted to be a hero for her, how much he'd wanted to fix everything for her.

They were no closer to finding the source of the threat against her, and maybe Kincaid and his men would have better luck figuring all this out. Troy recognized that it was time for him to bow out, but that didn't make it any less difficult.

"That's fine, whatever," she said, her mind obviously on other things. "Mike said it looked bad," she said, her worry for Big Sam deepening her voice.

"We'll know more when we get there," he replied. It would be particularly cruel of fate to take away Big Sam at this point in her life. She was already reeling from the absence of her father and the fact that somebody was trying to harm her. He sent up a silent plea that the dog be spared. She needed a break.

"He's got to be all right. He's just got to be. I was going to buy a house with a fenced yard. He was going to be my dog." She released a shuddering sigh that held suppressed tears.

Troy didn't reply. He had no words for her that would help.

It took twenty long minutes to get from the safe house to Precious Pets. When they pulled up in front of the building, the place looked deserted. No lights shone from the windows although Mike's truck was parked along the side of the building as it had been earlier that morning.

"He must be in the back," Brianna said as she got out of the car. "That's where the operating facility is."

She ran toward the front door and Troy hurried after her. Frantically she jabbed her key at the lock, her hand trembling so badly she had trouble hitting the hole. Troy took the keys from her and unlocked the door.

She threw it open and without bothering to turn on any lights raced toward the back room. Troy followed, the shimmer of moonlight drifting through the windows making her visible as she entered the kennel room.

Dogs began to bark and whine as she called to Mike, her cries barely audible above the din. An uneasiness filled Troy, but he tamped it down.

When she reached the back of the kennels, she came to a closed door. No light filtered out from beneath the door but she yanked it open anyway, then turned to look at Troy. "He's not here," she said. He saw the twist of grief and fear on her face. "Maybe we're too late. Maybe Big Sam is already dead."

"Don't jump to any conclusions. Let's go back outside. Mike's truck is still here. He's got to be around here someplace," he suggested.

She nodded and walked in front of him toward the front of the building. The uneasiness inside him grew. All his instincts began to scream that something wasn't right. But he didn't know if he was somehow reacting to a real threat of danger or to the emotional impact of the situation.

Where was Mike?

Where was Big Sam?

When he and Brianna had come in the front door, had Mike been carrying the dead dog out the back to load the body in the bed of his truck?

The constant barking was giving Troy a headache, making it difficult for him to think clearly. Mike had known they were on their way here, so where was he?

He was just ready to step out of the back room and back into the reception area when all the dogs seemed to stop barking to collect their breath for a second, and in that momentary silence, he thought he heard a footstep behind him.

He began to turn, but something slammed into

the back of his head with such force he crumbled to the floor. The last thing he heard was Brianna screaming his name—then nothing.

BRIANNA STOOD FROZEN and stared at Mike in the semidarkness of the room. Terror rose up inside her as she gazed at Troy's still, unmoving body. Mike stood over him, a metal bar in his hand.

"Mike?" Her mind grappled to make sense of what had just happened. Why would Mike attack Troy? It didn't make sense.

Mike threw the bar aside. It clattered to the floor as he pulled a gun from his pocket. "Hello, Bree."

A fierce trembling overtook her. Troy remained unmoving. Was he dead? Had the blow to his head killed him? She tore her gaze from Troy and once again looked at Mike. Why? What was going on? Why had he attacked Troy?

"Mike, what are you doing? What's going on? Wha…what do you want?" she asked.

He walked closer to her and pulled a length of rope from his pocket. "Right now I want you to shut up and turn around." The gun was pointed at her chest and there was no waver in his hand, no sense of hesitation in the brown depths of his eyes. She'd never known that brown eyes could be so cold, so empty of humanity.

She backed up and frantically looked around,

seeking a weapon, a means of escape, but there was nothing. And in any case she couldn't escape and leave Troy. He needed immediate medical attention…if he wasn't already dead. A sob welled up in the back of her throat at this thought, but she swallowed it. She couldn't think about that now. She couldn't think about Troy right now.

"I said turn around," Mike shouted.

She hesitated and then complied, the tone of his voice frightening her more than she'd ever been frightened in her life.

He tied her hands behind her back, then shoved her to the floor and used another piece of rope to tie her feet together.

"Why are you doing this? Mike, talk to me." She felt as if she'd walked into a nightmare, one that made no sense, that she couldn't figure out but that terrified her.

He used another length of rope to tie her bound ankles to the foot of the receptionist desk, then stood and smiled down at her. "We'll talk when I get back. First I have to take the trash out." He gestured toward Troy.

"Leave him alone," she cried, tears welling up in her eyes. "Whatever is wrong, it's between me and you. Mike, just leave him out of it." The words tore from her throat in a savage scream.

"Shut up," he yelled. He stuffed his gun in his waistband, then walked over to Troy and picked up his feet. He began to drag Troy's body across the floor and out the front door.

When he was gone, a deep sob escaped Brianna and she began to struggle to get free of the ropes that bound her. But he'd tied them with the purpose of keeping her captive. The knots were tight and with her hands behind her back, it was impossible to free her legs.

As she struggled, her mind raced. She'd never done anything to Mike except treat him with respect, as a valuable member of her team. Why was he doing this? What could this possibly be about?

And what about Troy? If he wasn't already dead, did Mike intend to kill him? Where was Mike taking him? The full horror of what was happening was just beginning to sink in.

She pulled with her legs against the desk, but the desk was too heavy to move. If she could reach the phone on top maybe she could knock the receiver off the hook and use her tongue to punch in 911.

With tears half-blinding her, she tried to sit up enough to reach the top of the desk. Her tears stopped momentarily as she focused on maneuvering her body into position. But she began a new round of weeping as she managed a look on the desktop and saw that the phone had been removed.

At least she hadn't heard a gunshot. Although she realized it was possible that Mike didn't have to shoot Troy, that Troy was already dead.

It was all her fault. He had nothing to do with this.

He'd simply been pulled into this mess by doing a favor for a fellow ex-Navy man. When her father had been kidnapped she should have insisted that he drop the case. If she'd done that he'd be fine right now.

Had Mike killed her father? Once again she was back to trying to make sense of it all. Why? If he was going to kill her, she just hoped she knew the reason before she died.

Minutes ticked by, agonizing minutes of waiting, of watching the doorway for his return. She continued to try to get free from the ropes but made no progress in untying the tight knots. The dogs in the back room had quieted, and she was left only with her own thoughts.

She wished she'd come home from California a year ago, two years ago. She'd lost so much time with her father, time that she would probably never reclaim. How she desperately wished she'd put that part of her life behind her, exchanged the designer gowns and paparazzi for jeans and family photos.

And she wished she'd told Troy she loved him.

Even though she knew he didn't love her back, at least not in the way she loved him, she wished she would have said the words to him, let him know that she thought he was a wonderful man.

She didn't want to die, felt as if she hadn't truly begun living. She'd had so many plans for her life, plans that she'd just been beginning to realize.

Her breath caught in her throat as Mike reappeared in the doorway. On his pleasant, average face, she saw a hatred she didn't understand, a hatred that she knew was deadly.

"What did you do to Troy? Where have you taken him?" she asked, her voice sounding pathetically weak and reedy to her own ears. "Damn you," she exclaimed, her voice stronger as rage filled her. "What have you done with him?"

He merely smiled. "We don't have to worry about him anymore. He won't be playing the white knight and rushing to save you. Nobody is going to save you, Brianna. It's just you and me now."

She stared at him in horror.

Troy REGAINED CONSCIOUSNESS in bits and pieces, the back of his head screaming with pain. All he wanted to do was go back to sleep, back to the darkness where pain hadn't existed, but beneath the pain simmered an urgency that refused to allow him the pleasure of drifting into unconsciousness again.

He lay on his back and slowly became aware of the scent of grass and an unpleasant odor of animal surrounding him. Why was he outside? He opened his eyes and stared into nothing. No stars. No moon. Nothing but an impenetrable blackness.

He frowned, the gesture shooting a sharp stab of pain through his skull. Where was he? What had happened? Again the darkness called, beckoning him with a siren song to fall into it, to release his tenuous hold on consciousness. But he fought against it and pulled himself into a sitting position.

Brianna. Her name shot through him and suddenly everything came tumbling back. Big Sam. The phone call from Mike. Mike! Troy reached up a hand and touched the back of his head. Although incredibly painful and sporting a large lump, there didn't seem to be any blood.

Brianna! What was happening to her?

He struggled to get to his feet and his head slammed into a low ceiling he hadn't known was there. Where was he? Crouched down, he swept a hand out and encountered a wooden wall.

He moved several steps forward, still exploring with his hands. His hand touched a bag of some kind and like a blind person explored it by touch. It was a large bag, opened at the top, and as he felt the dry nuggets that it contained he realized it was dog food.

So he must be in a storage shed of some kind. His foot connected with something and he heard a low moan.

He nearly shot out of his skin as he realized wherever he was, he wasn't alone. "Who's there?" he asked, his body poised with fight or flight adrenaline.

Another moan filled the air. Troy leaned down to see what his foot had connected with and as he reached out he touched a man's shoe. The shoe was on a foot, and the foot belonged to a body that shared the space with him. A live body.

"Brandon?" he guessed.

"Help me."

The voice was pitifully weak but Troy recognized it as Brandon Waverly's. He was alive! Thank God. "It's me, Brandon. It's Troy. It's all right," he said. "You're going to be okay."

"Troy? Drugged, can't get up. Weak as a baby," Brandon muttered.

Troy crawled in the direction of Brandon's head. "Are you hurt?"

"No, just so weak. How'd you find me? Who did this?"

"You don't know?" Troy asked.

"Never saw him…the man who took me. He wore a mask. He's kept me drugged, but I've never seen his face, never heard his voice."

"It was Mike, the veterinarian who works at Precious Pets," Troy replied.

Troy worked his hands around the perimeter and realized the wooden structure that held them was small but tightly built.

He found the hinges and the fastening of the door, but it was locked. He pushed against it, but felt no give. His head banged with a nauseating intensity. Think. He had to think. There had to be a way out. He had to get to Brianna.

"Troy," Brandon's weak voice called from the darkness. "If you're in here with me, then where is our girl? Where's Brianna?"

Troy threw himself against the door once again, trying to break through the lock that held them captive. He didn't answer Brandon. He couldn't tell the man that while he and Brandon were trapped inside here, his daughter was out there with a madman.

Chapter Thirteen

"You thought you could just waltz back here and take over?" Mike bent down to untie her from the desk leg. "You really thought you could spend all this time in Hollywood partying and then decide to come back here and run the business I've put my sweat and blood in?"

Brianna stared at his twisted features in stunned surprise. "That's what this is all about? You're afraid you won't be in charge here at Precious Pets?" A hysterical laugh nearly left her lips, but she bit it back, afraid of his reaction.

He got her loose from the desk, then worked on the ropes that bound her ankles together. He shook his head and gave her a sly smile. "You don't know everything that goes on here. You and your daddy were going to screw things up for me. If you'd just died in that nightclub in California, then none of this would be necessary."

Brianna gasped. "You? You tried to kill me in that nightclub?"

He laughed, a sharp bark of sound that held no humor. "If it had been me, you'd be dead. Unfortunately, I left the job to a business associate of mine and he didn't get the job done."

"But why? I don't understand." She twisted her legs away from him, wanting to buy herself time, wanting to get some answers that made sense. "If you want me dead, then at least tell me why."

He sat back on his haunches, obviously not worried about anyone coming to her aid. And who would? It was the middle of the night. They were in the middle of nowhere and for all she knew Troy was dead. She shoved this thought aside, knowing that if she dwelled on it she'd go mad.

She had to keep her wits about her. She had to figure out how to get out of this, a way to escape, and she couldn't do that with despair, with mind-numbing grief clouding her thoughts.

"Do you have any idea how much money can be made selling designer dogs? Those little hybrid pets that you women in Hollywood carry around like accessories? It's a huge business and I've been cashing in. Back in the woods I've got a million dollar business going on, and you and your father were about to screw it all up."

He grabbed her legs once again and held them tight. "I knew I could slow down the mall development long enough to find another place to conduct my business, but then you showed up here with the sudden decision to be a part of all this." The words spat out of him.

"It was easy to get everyone stirred up about the mall development. All I had to do was get that nut Stafford involved, and I knew I'd buy myself some time. Then you came back to town and I knew I needed to get more creative. I figured if your father was kidnapped, you'd be so busy you wouldn't have time to think about Precious Pets. But I knew you were a problem that needed to be taken care of permanently." His face twisted with rage once again. "I can't have you here. This place is mine. That business is mine."

Her head reeled with all the information he was spewing. He'd taken her father? He was selling designer dogs? She wanted to ask what he'd done to her father, but she was afraid of what the answer might be. In any case if she didn't manage to get away from him, it wouldn't matter what he'd done to her dad. She knew Mike intended to kill her.

"Then it was you who tried to run me over the night of the meeting?" she asked, still trying to buy more time.

"I didn't plan that. I borrowed a car from a friend, and all I wanted to do was follow you and your boyfriend to wherever you were staying, but then you appeared in the middle of the road, all alone, and I just stepped on the gas."

What she didn't understand was why he just didn't shoot her now. Nobody would hear the shot. As he untied her feet, she summoned all the strength she had in her legs and kicked at his face.

She connected with his chin and he reeled backward, cursing her as she frantically got to her feet. She raced for the front door but screamed as he grabbed her by the hair and yanked her backward.

"Scream all you want, Bree. Nobody can hear you," he said with a laugh as he tightened his grip on her hair. He pulled her up against the length of his body, the barrel of the gun jabbed just beneath her chin.

"I'd shoot you now, but I don't want to clean up the mess. We're going to take a little drive to your daddy's job site. Eventually somebody will find your body there, and they'll think it was one of the locals or that Stafford guy. Or maybe I'll just shoot you and cut you up, feed you to the dogs here and nobody will ever know what happened to you."

He began to maneuver her toward the open front door. She knew if he managed to get her outside the building she was as good as dead. He tucked the gun back in his waistband, and for just a brief moment, he released his hold on her hair. She spun around and shoved his body with hers, catching him off guard, and he stumbled backward and halfway to the floor.

She ran not toward the front door but for the back room where there was an outside door. If she couldn't make it there, there were plenty of places to hide.

As she entered, the dogs began to bark and bay, as if sensing her terror, as if responding to her emotional stress. They jumped at their cage doors as she ran down first one aisle, then another.

"You can't get away," Mike yelled from behind her.

He'd see her if she went out the door, and she knew he wouldn't hesitate to put a bullet in her back. With sheer desperation when she reached the third aisle, she crawled into one of the empty cages and held her breath, hoping…praying for a miracle.

She held her breath and wished she could hear where Mike was, but the noise of the dogs that would make it difficult for him to hear her also made it difficult for her to hear his approach.

She'd never known such fear as what coursed through her now. Her blood had turned to ice and her heart crashed so hard against her ribs, she felt as if she might be sick.

The overhead lights flipped on. "Bree." Mike's laughter rose above the din. "I always win at hide-and-seek." She heard the sound of cage doors opening and then slamming shut.

Oh God, he was going to find her. He was going to find her and then kill her. She pressed farther back into the large cage, the steel bars digging into her back, and shoved her fist against her lips to stay the scream that fought to be released.

Minutes passed, agonizing minutes of silence. The dogs were quieting again but she couldn't hear Mike, had no idea where he might be.

She pressed her fist harder against her mouth. She'd

run herself into a corner where there was no way out. She had doomed herself by crawling into the cage.

It was only when Mike's face peered at her from outside the iron bars that she released the scream that she'd tried desperately to hold inside.

THE PAIN IN HIS HEAD had eased to a dull throb, making it easier to think more clearly. It took Troy only an instant to realize that Mike must have frisked him after dumping him here. His cell phone was gone as was his wallet. He'd probably been looking for a gun, but he hadn't thought about checking Troy's ankle. The gun rested against his skin, and after throwing himself at the gate in an attempt to get it open, Troy drew the weapon.

He hoped he wouldn't have to use it. He didn't want Mike to hear the gunfire and realize he was not only conscious but also armed.

Troy would have preferred a sneak attack, but the minutes were ticking by, minutes that might mean life and death for Brianna.

"I'll be back for you, Brandon," he said in the darkness. "I promise everything is going to be all right."

He used his fingers to feel where he thought the lock was on the outside of the structure, then he placed the barrel of the gun against the wood and fired.

The lock shot away and the gate opened. Troy pushed through it and fell to his knees outside in the moonlight. He got to his feet and looked around.

He was in the middle of a small clearing that was surrounded by trees and brush. He wasn't alone in the clearing.

Stunned, he stared at the cages, one on top of another, and all of them filled with tiny puppies. A puppy mill. That's what this had been about. There were several larger pens, and in one stood a perfectly healthy Big Sam.

Troy turned in all four directions, trying to get a handle on exactly where he was. He had to be at the back of the Precious Pets property. He gazed up at the moon to get his bearings, then took off at a run.

He had no idea how long he'd been unconscious. It could have been minutes or it could have been an hour. He might be too late. This thought made his legs work faster.

His heart kept a steady beat as a cool calm descended over him. It was the calm of prebattle.

If Mike had hurt Brianna, then Troy would hunt him down. All his military training came back in a rush as he slid around trees and across brush and grass without making a sound.

The building came into view, the back of it blazing with lights. He clutched his gun more tightly. He wouldn't hesitate to shoot if necessary. He would kill Mike Kidwell to save Brianna's life and not blink an eye in the process.

He slid up to the back of the building and tried the

back door. Locked. His jaw clenched tight, he moved like a shadow across the back and heard the sound of a truck roar to life.

He jumped around the corner of the building in time to see Mike behind the wheel in his pickup. "Kidwell!" he shouted.

Mike stepped on the gas, the back tires spewing up gravel and dust as he shot forward. Troy took a stance and aimed his gun at the truck. He fired three times and the last bullet blew out the front tire on the driver's side.

The truck careened out of control down the lane and straight across the street where it struck a tree head-on with a loud bang. The engine cut off and an eerie silence filled the night.

Only then did Troy's heart begin to beat a frantic rhythm. He had no idea if Brianna was in the truck or back at Precious Pets. He had no idea if she were dead or alive.

With his gun still clutched in his hand, he approached the truck cautiously. As he drew closer he saw Mike slumped over the steering wheel, but Brianna wasn't sitting in the passenger seat.

His heart clenched tightly, making it difficult for him to draw a breath. Had Mike already killed Brianna and been making his getaway?

He got to the driver's window and reached out to see if there was a pulse in Mike's neck. As Troy touched him, the man released a low, deep moan, letting Troy know he was alive.

"Where's Brianna?" he asked, but Mike didn't move.

"Troy?"

Her voice came from the passenger side and he saw her then, curled up in front of the seat on the floor. "Brianna." Her name exploded out of him with relief.

He hurried to the passenger door and yanked it open. She fell out into his arms. "I thought you were dead," she said as she cried. "Oh God, I thought he'd killed you."

Troy hugged her, relief bringing a sheen of tears to his eyes, then he released her. "Turn around and let me untie your hands."

She whirled around and he managed to get the rope off her. Mike had begun to moan again, and knowing how dangerous he could be, Troy took the rope from Brianna's hands and returned to the driver's side of the truck.

He pushed Mike back from the steering wheel. The man's face was bloody and it was obvious he'd made hard contact with the steering wheel when they'd crashed.

Troy quickly went through his pockets, finding a gun, a cell phone and his wallet. He took all three items and handed them to Brianna, then tied Mike's hands to the steering wheel.

He took the phone and called 911, then Brianna was in his arms once again. He held her tightly as she trembled against him. The warmth of her, the scent of her filled him with a weary relief.

"It's over," he murmured into her hair. "It's really, finally over."

"He was selling dogs, expensive designer dogs. He sent somebody to try to kill me in Hollywood. He was behind it all." The words tumbled from her, as if it were important that Troy know everything she'd learned. She looked up at him, her eyes haunted in the moonlight. "We thought it was because of my lifestyle or my dad's work, but it was about Precious Pets and money."

"I know. I saw the puppies out in the woods. And I saw something else, Brianna." He held tight to her, glad that he was about to take that haunted look from her eyes. "I saw your father. He's alive. Big Sam, too."

He watched her face, captured that moment of joy that crossed her features in his memory and knew that when this was over Brianna Waverly would take away a tiny piece of his heart.

Chapter Fourteen

The sun had peeked over the horizon an hour earlier and exhaustion weighed heavily on Brianna's shoulders. The night had passed in a blur. The police had arrived along with several news crews. Two ambulances arrived, one for Mike and one for her father.

The initial assessment of Brandon had been that he was dehydrated and weak as a baby. He was suffering the effects of a tranquilizer, but he was going to be okay.

Mike had a concussion and a broken nose from hitting the steering wheel, but he'd suffered no other injuries and would live to stand trial for enough crimes to keep him in prison for a very long time.

Brianna now stood in front of the cages in the clearing, her heart aching as she saw the terrible condition the little puppies had been living in. The cages were filthy and overcrowded. Some of the puppies were healthy and bright-eyed, but others were sick and listless.

Seventy-six puppies. She'd counted them. Not only did the clearing contain the cages, but the police had also found dogfighting training equipment and a cage of pit bulls. Apparently Mike had meant to branch out into breeding and training pit bulls.

"You've got your work cut out for you."

She whirled around at the sound of the deep voice and offered a tired smile to Chief Kincaid. "This wasn't exactly the kind of publicity I wanted for Precious Pets." She looked back at the cages. "And yes, I have my work cut out for me. It's hard to believe that a man who was trained to save animals would do something like this."

"Money. It all comes down to the mighty dollar. I just got an update from the hospital. Mike is conscious and spilling his guts. He told my officers that he didn't intend on killing anyone. He'd kidnapped your father to slow things down with the mall development and he just wanted to scare you a little bit."

"Yeah, right. And I like bling just a little bit," she replied dryly.

"We're trying to hunt down the name of his associate in California. We've taken custody of his home computer, and I have a feeling we're going to find plenty of answers there, both about this business he was running and any associates he might have had."

"I'm just grateful that my father is going to be all right and nobody got seriously hurt." She released a weary sigh and once again looked at the puppies. "As for these little guys, I'm going to get in touch with a couple of agencies and see if they can help me. My goal is to get them cleaned up, healthy and adopted out to good homes."

"We've already gotten some calls from people who saw the story on the news and want to know how they can help," Wendall said.

"Maybe he wasn't going to kill my father, but no matter what he's saying now I'm certain he intended to kill both me and Troy."

"And he'll be charged with attempted murder," Wendall replied.

At that moment Troy entered the clearing. He looked as tired as she felt. He offered her a smile, then glanced at the wooden structure where he'd been held and where Brandon had been found. It had apparently been built to hold supplies.

"If Mike had found my gun, Brandon and I would still be locked in that box," he said. He didn't add that if he hadn't gotten out of that box she would be dead.

"I told you that ankle holster was very James Bond," Brianna said with a touch of humor.

Troy's gray eyes lightened, then he looked at Wendall. "Are we done here for now? I think what Brianna and I need most right now is some sleep."

Wendall nodded. "You're done. If we have any more questions we'll give you a call. In the meantime get some sleep. It's been a long night." With a nod to each of them he turned and left the clearing.

It was the first time Brianna and Troy had been alone since the police had arrived. She wanted to walk into his arms, feel the steady beat of his heart against her own.

"I was so afraid for you," she said, but didn't move closer to him.

He jammed his hands in his pockets. "No more than I was for you," he replied.

"It's hard to believe it's over." It was even harder to believe that it was time to tell him goodbye. After all they'd been through, after all they had shared, the idea of never seeing him again filled her with an overwhelming grief.

"Are you ready to get out of here?" he asked.

She began to say yes and then stopped, knowing that she had to tell him how she felt. "Not quite," she said and took a couple of steps closer to him. "If I don't tell you something right now, I'll live with regret for the rest of my life, and I'm not a woman who likes regret."

He tensed, his shoulders stiffening and the muscle in his jaw knotting. His eyes narrowed slightly and he pulled his hands from his pockets. "Brianna, it's been a hell of a night. I'm exhausted and just want to get out of here. Whatever you want to say, can't it wait until another time?"

"No. This will just take a minute." She took another step toward him, close enough now that she could see the blond morning stubble on his jaw, smell the achingly familiar scent of his cologne.

She wanted to find just the right words, needed him to know that she wasn't reacting from the trauma of the night or the heat of the moment.

"I'm in love with you." The oh-so-simple words fell from her lips. Emotion pressed thickly against her chest.

She wasn't sure what she expected his reaction to be, but it wasn't his lips compressing tightly together or the step backward he took from her. She'd hoped for a truly romantic moment. She'd hoped that he would take her in his arms and tell her he loved her, too, that he couldn't imagine his life without her in it.

But it wasn't the joy of realized love that crossed his features. Rather, it was an uncomfortable dismay that broke her heart.

"You don't have to say anything," she exclaimed, fighting against the tears that welled up inside her. "I know I'm not your fantasy woman. I think you liked Brianna Waverly, but you have no tolerance for Bree, and the problem is that I'm both. I won't apologize for the way I lived my life in California. I loved my life while I was there. It's part of who I am. I'm not timid or shy. I like beer and pizza and I love a pair of worn jeans, but I also like champagne and caviar and designer clothes. I'm not a simple woman. I'm complicated."

She was surprised to feel the splash of tears on her cheeks. "What's worse is I think you love me, too. But you have this fantasy woman in your mind and she's the one you want." The words tumbled out of her, as if she'd been waiting a lifetime to speak them and now had her chance.

"I haven't figured it out yet, if it's fear or selfishness that has kept you single, that has kept you clinging to some mysterious woman who might not even exist. But I'm real and I'm here and I love you. I just wanted you to know that. Now I'm ready to leave."

She turned and headed out of the clearing, hoping…praying that he'd call to her, tell her he was as much in love with her as she was with him.

The tears fell faster as he followed silently behind her. They reached her vehicle and got in. The exhaustion that had weighed her down was nothing compared to the heartache she now carried with her.

"I'll drop you at your father's house and then one of my partners will get your car and your things from the safe house back to you later this afternoon," he said once they were headed away from Precious Pets.

"Whatever," she replied. He hadn't even acknowledged what she'd said to him. She felt as if she'd just professed her love to a rock.

The silence continued until he pulled up in front of the Waverly mansion. She unbuckled her seat belt and started to get out but he stopped her by grabbing her arm.

For just a moment a rich, ripe hope swept through her. Maybe he'd just needed time to process what she'd said to him.

"Brianna, I just want you to know that you're a

terrific woman and someday you'll find a terrific guy to share your life." His eyes were the flat gray of an overcast sky.

The last little bit of hope that had lived inside her died at his words. "But that terrific guy isn't you."

He released his hold on her arm. "We've been through a traumatic experience. I think once you get alone with yourself you'll realize that what you feel for me is gratitude and the bond of a victim for a protector, but it isn't real love."

"Thank you for sharing with me how *I* feel." She opened the car door and stepped out. "Have a nice life, Troy. I hope you find what you're looking for."

Half-blinded by tears, Brianna walked to the front door and rang the bell. The door hadn't even opened before she heard the sound of him pulling out of the driveway.

She had tons of things to think about. She had seventy-six puppies that needed to be cleaned up and found homes, she had to make amends with Heather and go visit her father in the hospital. She'd be far too busy to waste another minute of thought on Troy and what might have been. That's what she told herself as the housekeeper let her inside.

That's what she told herself as she made her way up the grand staircase and into her bedroom. She threw herself on the bed and tried to convince herself that her heart wasn't broken, that she didn't care that she loved Troy Sinclair and he didn't love her back.

THE NEXT TWO WEEKS flew by for Brianna. She arranged for her things in California to be packed up and moved back to Kansas City. From dawn until dusk, she worked at Precious Pets. With the help of a veterinarian who donated his time and half a dozen volunteers, they managed to get all the puppies washed, healthy and placed in either foster homes or with rescue agencies until they could be properly adopted.

Her father remembered little of his time imprisoned in the storage shelter. Mike had kept him drugged most of the time, providing just enough water and food to keep him alive. Mike had never intended to kill Brandon. He'd meant only to hold him long enough to postpone any work at the mall until he could move his operation someplace else. But before he'd made arrangements to do that, Brianna had let him know she was returning to Kansas City permanently. So she'd become an immediate threat that needed to be taken care of.

Heather graciously accepted Brianna's apology for suspecting her, and Brianna thought that the two of them would remain friends long after Heather's divorce from Brandon was finalized.

But as busy as she stayed, as warm and welcoming as friends and family had been following everything that had happened, her heart still held the shattering that Troy had left behind.

It was just after eight on a beautiful Saturday morning when she arrived at Precious Pets. Big Sam greeted her, bounding out to her car with enough tail wags to nearly lift him off the ground.

"Hi, buddy," she said and patted him on the head as he accompanied her into the building.

Sandy greeted her with a bright smile. "Morning, boss," she said. "I've got coffee made and three families scheduled this morning to come in about adopting."

"Wonderful." Brianna went to the back room to check on the animals. As she went from cage to cage, murmuring greetings and giving each pet a scratch behind the ear or a pat on the head, she thought of the new relationship she and Sandy were starting to build. It was one based on mutual respect and a growing friendship.

"If you can man the front for an hour or so, I'm going to bring that schnauzer that came in yesterday in for a bath and a groom," Sandy said.

"Not a problem." Brianna poured herself a cup of coffee and sat in the chair behind the desk. She sipped her coffee and stared out the window. As always when her mind had a moment of quiet time, her thoughts sifted through the events of the last two weeks.

Mike's associate in California had been identified and arrested and would stand trial for the attack that had injured her bodyguard.

She'd met Kent for lunch and had explained everything that had happened. During that lunch date, she'd recognized that Troy had been right. Kent was in love with her, so while they ate, she made it clear that he would never be the man in her life, that it was time for him to move on and find a nice woman who wanted to share his life.

Funny, how you could break somebody's heart when that wasn't your intention. She never wanted to break Kent's and she knew that it had never been Troy's intention to break hers.

She supposed the next time she saw Troy would be at Mike's trial, when they'd both be testifying against the man who had wanted them dead.

Would her heartache have lessened by then? Somehow she believed that part of her heart would always be damaged by loving Troy, that there would always be a broken piece that no amount of time, that no new love, would ever be able to heal.

The morning passed with a flurry of activity as the three families showed up to view the dogs and Brianna fielded phone calls. She had begun receiving applications from veterinarians and spent part of the time reading over those and looking for somebody who would be a good fit.

It was almost one when she sent Sandy to lunch. "I'm going to that chicken place off the highway. Want me to bring something back for you?" Sandy asked.

"No thanks, I'm not really hungry. I'll just plan on an early dinner tonight," Brianna replied.

"I'll be back within an hour," Sandy said.

"Take your time. I've got things covered here."

Brianna watched as the young woman left the building and got into her car.

She leaned back in her chair and opened the newspaper to the real estate section. At the moment she was staying with her father, but she hoped to buy her own house as soon as possible, a house with a big fenced yard for Big Sam.

"Here we go, buddy, a story and a half with granite countertops in the kitchen, a hot tub and a fenced yard." She reached down and patted Sam, who lay on the floor snoozing next to her chair. "What do you think, Big Sam, does a hot tub float your boat?"

As she heard the sound of a car on the gravel road, she put the paper aside and glanced out the window. Her stomach clenched as she recognized the little sports car pulling up in front of the building.

She watched in disbelief as Troy climbed out of the driver's seat, his buzz-cut blond hair sparkling in the sunshine. What was he doing here? Self-consciously she swept a hand through her hair, then realizing what she was doing, she quickly dropped her hand to the top of the desk.

Maybe she'd left something at the safe house and he'd come to return it. Or maybe something had come up about the case that he needed to discuss with her.

Still, she couldn't stop the way her heart tattooed in her chest at the sight of him, the way she felt half-breathless and flushed as she watched him walk with determined strides to the door.

She didn't know how long it took to heal a wounded heart, but two weeks wasn't long enough. She steeled herself as he opened the door and walked in, bringing with him that familiar scent that twisted her heart even more.

"Well, well, look who's here," she said, pleased that her voice betrayed none of the emotions his presence evoked in her.

"Hi, Brianna. You're looking well."

"Thanks. You don't look so bad yourself." In truth, he looked amazing. As usual, he was clad in a pair of navy slacks that fit his long, lean legs to perfection. The short-sleeved white dress shirt he wore fit his broad shoulders and displayed the corded muscles of his arms—arms she wanted around her at this very moment.

"I've heard through the grapevine that you got the puppy thing all cleaned up," he said.

She nodded. "I had a lot of help. People stepped up to volunteer and we managed to place all of them." Frustration welled up inside her. She couldn't stand it any longer. She got up from the desk. "What are you doing here, Troy?"

He stepped closer to her and she wished she could read the expression in his beautiful gray eyes, but she couldn't.

"I've come to adopt," he said.

She stared at him in surprise. "Oh." He'd never mentioned wanting an animal before and it would have been so much easier if he'd gone to the pound. Why did he have to come here, to her, knowing how she felt about him, knowing how he didn't feel about her. Thick emotion swelled in her chest.

She pulled an adoption form from the desk drawer, hoping she could get through this without crying. "What did you have in mind?"

"Blond," he said. "Definitely a blonde. And she has to be complicated and with a touch of a stubborn streak."

She stared at him, wondering if this was some sort of a cruel joke or if maybe she misunderstood what he was saying.

He took another step toward her. "She needs to like blue jeans and designer shoes, hot dogs with relish and caviar."

Her. He was talking about her. Her heart sounded a drumbeat of joy. "I have one in particular that I think would be perfect for you," she said. "But I think she might need a little obedience training."

The corners of his mouth lifted in a smile that warmed her from head to toe. "Oh no, I'm crazy about her just the way she is and I can't imagine my life without her…."

He got no other words out of his mouth before she launched herself into his arms. "You have to be talking about me because I know for a fact that all the dogs I have up for adoption positively hate designer shoes."

He wrapped his arms around her. "I'm definitely talking about you."

"What about that fantasy woman you've been carrying around in your head all this time?" she asked.

His smile faltered and he gazed down at her with love and tenderness as he tightened his arms around her. "You told me that you weren't sure if it was fear or selfishness that kept me clinging to that fantasy. For the past two weeks, that question has haunted me."

He stroked a hand through her hair, his eyes so warm, so inviting, she knew she could look at them forever. "Fear," he said. "You scared me to death. I've never felt this way about anyone before. I was terrified that you'd break my heart, but I realized over the last couple of days that my heart was broken anyway, because I'd pushed you out of my life."

"I can't change who I am, Troy," she said softly. "There's a little bit of Bree inside me, and she's not going anywhere."

He smiled again. "I love that woman. I love you, woman." He kissed her then, and in his kiss she knew that Brianna Waverly had left Hollywood behind forever, because she'd found what she'd been looking for in Troy Sinclair's arms.

* * * * *

Celebrate 60 years of pure reading
pleasure with Harlequin®!

Harlequin Presents® *is proud to introduce*
its gripping new miniseries,
THE ROYAL HOUSE OF KAREDES.
An exquisite coronation diamond, split as a
symbol of a warring royal family's feud,
is missing! But whoever reunites the
diamond halves will rule all....

Welcome to eight brand-new titles that unfold
to reveal the stories of kings and queens,
princes and princesses torn apart by pride
and power, but finally reunited by love.

Step into the world of Karedes with
BILLIONAIRE PRINCE, PREGNANT MISTRESS
Available July 2009
from Harlequin Presents®.

ALEXANDROS KAREDES, SNOW DUSTING the shoulders of his leather jacket and glittering like jewels in his dark hair, stood at the door. Maria felt the blood drain from her head.

"Good evening, Ms. Santos."

His voice was as she remembered it. Deep. Husky. Perfect English, but with the faintest hint of a Greek accent. And cold, as cold as it had been that awful morning she would never forget, when he'd accused her of horrible things, called her terrible names....

"Aren't you going to ask me in?"

She fought for composure. Last time they'd faced each other, they'd been on his turf. Now they were on hers. She was in command here, and that meant everything.

"There's a sign on the door downstairs," she said, her tone every bit as frigid as his. "It says, 'No soliciting or vagrants.'"

His lips drew back in a wolfish grin. "Very amusing."

"What do you want, Prince Alexandros?"

A tight smile eased across his mouth and it killed her that even now, knowing he was a vicious, arrogant man, she couldn't help but notice what a handsome mouth it was. Chiseled. Generous. Beautiful, like the rest of him, which made him living proof that beauty could, indeed, be only skin deep.

"Such formality, Maria. You were hardly so proper the last time we were together."

She knew his choice of words was deliberate. She felt her face heat; she couldn't help that but she damned well didn't have to let him lure her into a verbal sparring match.

"I'll ask you once more, your highness. What do you want?"

"Ask me in and I'll tell you."

"I have no intention of asking you in. Tell me why you're here or don't. It's your choice, just as it will be my choice to shut the door in your face."

He laughed. It infuriated her but she could hardly blame him. He was tall—six-two, six-three—and though he stood with one shoulder leaning against the door frame, hands tucked casually into the pockets of the jacket, his pose was deceptive. He was strong, with the leanly muscled body of a well-trained athlete.

She remembered his body with painful clarity. The feel of him under her hands. The power of him moving over her. The taste of him on her tongue.

Suddenly, he straightened, his laughter gone. "I have not come this distance to stand in your doorway," he said coldly, "and I am not going to leave until I am ready to do so. I suggest you stand aside and stop behaving like a petulant child."

A petulant child? Was that what he thought? This man who had spent hours making love to her and had then accused her of—of trading her body for profit?

Except it had not been love, it had been sex. And the sooner she got rid of him, the better.

She let go of the doorknob and stepped aside. "You have five minutes."

He strolled past her, bringing cold air and the scent of the night with him. She swung toward him, arms folded. He reached past her, pushed the door closed, then folded his arms, too. She wanted to open the door again but she'd be damned if she was going to get into a who's-in-charge-here argument with him. She was in charge, and he would surely see a tussle over the ground rules as a sign of weakness.

Instead, she looked past him at the big clock above her worktable.

"Ten seconds gone," she said briskly. "You're wasting time, your highness."

"What I have to say will take longer than five minutes."

"Then you'll just have to learn to economize. More than five minutes, I'll call the police."

Instantly, his hand was wrapped around her wrist. He tugged her toward him, his dark-chocolate eyes almost black with anger.

"You do that and I'll tell every tabloid shark I can contact about how Maria Santos tried to buy a five-hundred-thousand-dollar commission by seducing a prince." He smiled thinly. "They'll lap it up."

* * * * *

What will it take for this
billionaire prince to realize he's
falling in love with his mistress…?
Look for
BILLIONAIRE PRINCE, PREGNANT MISTRESS
by Sandra Marton
Available July 2009
from Harlequin Presents®.

In 2009 Harlequin celebrates
60 years of pure reading pleasure!

We're marking this occasion by offering
16 **FREE** full books to download and read.

We invite you to visit and share the Web site
with your friends, family
and anyone who enjoys reading.

You're invited to join our Tell Harlequin Reader Panel!

By joining our new reader panel you will:

- Receive Harlequin® books—they are FREE and yours to keep with no obligation to purchase anything!
- Participate in fun online surveys
- Exchange opinions and ideas with women just like you
- Have a say in our new book ideas and help us publish the best in women's fiction

In addition, you will have a chance to win great prizes and receive special gifts!
See Web site for details. Some conditions apply.
Space is limited.

To join, visit us at
www.TellHarlequin.com.

REQUEST YOUR FREE BOOKS!

2 FREE NOVELS PLUS 2 FREE GIFTS!

HARLEQUIN®

INTRIGUE®

Breathtaking Romantic Suspense

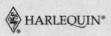